WHAT HE WAS DOING TO HER SENSES WAS ADDICTIVE

One stroke demanded another, one caress a second. Though she'd always prided herself on being in control, Greg awakened a stunning hunger.

Suddenly, though, he pulled back. Taking in slow, unsteady breaths, he looked down at the flush on her lips, and the moistness he'd left in her eyes. Oh, yes, he'd aroused her. But she'd also done a damned good job of arousing *him*, and that hadn't been part of the scheme.

Lowering his gaze, he focused on the necklace and not for the first time wondered what power it held.

DELINSKY

FULFILMENT

MIRA BOOKS

All the characters in this book have no existence outside the imagination
of the author, and have no relation whatsoever to anyone bearing the
same name or names. They are not even distantly inspired by any
individual known or unknown to the author, and all the incidents are pure
invention.

First published in Great Britain 1989
Reprinted in Great Britain 1995
by Mira Books

© Barbara Delinsky 1988

ISBN 1 55166 026 1

58-9508

Printed in Great Britain by
BPC Paperbacks Ltd

1

When Diandra Casey's plane was ninety minutes late landing, she feared it was an omen. When she swept through the door of Bartholomew York's spacious penthouse apartment to find Gregory York there, she knew it had been one.

Gregory York was her nemesis. Her first memory of him was when she'd been three and he eight, when he'd lured her into the boxwood labyrinth at his parents' Bar Harbor estate and abandoned her there. Just as she'd learned not to play with fire, she'd learned to be wary of Gregory, and if she'd been able to avoid him completely in the years subsequent to the labyrinth incident, she'd have done so.

It hadn't been possible. The link between their families was complex. Not only were their parents best of friends, but their grandparents—and great-grandparents—had been, as well. Ties dated back to the turn of the century, when Diandra's great-grandfather, Malcolm Casey, had teamed up with Greg's great-grandfather, Henry York, to open a small general store. That general store had grown into a small department store, which had grown into a larger department store, which had grown into two, then three, then more. CayCorp had evolved, and the posh chain known as Casey and York, with branches in the most select and sophisticated of cities, rivaled none.

Within CayCorp, though, there were rivals galore. Each of the seven stores was run by a Casey or a York, and while much good-natured competitive banter flew between them, all banter stopped with the appearance of the annual report. Bartholomew York, chairman of the board and patriarch of the families, read the report cover to cover. He noted how successful each branch was, and if one wasn't performing up to par, he wanted to know why.

No one argued with Old Bart. He'd been around too long and had proved his worth too many times for that. He was a shrewd businessman with an eye for character, which was why, once she'd completed her M.B.A. and an apprenticeship under her father, who ran the Chicago store, Diandra had been named a vice president of CayCorp and put in charge of the Washington, D.C., store. She'd been only twenty-seven at the time, but she'd shown the kind of drive that Bart liked. In the five years since then, she'd successfully rejuvenated that branch of Casey and York that had begun to stagnate.

Gregory had the trend-setting New York store. His job was to keep it in the forefront of high fashion, and for the past ten years he'd succeeded admirably—so much so that Diandra knew he had something up his sleeve. She also knew what it was.

He wanted San Francisco.

For two years, Old Bart had been making noises about opening a branch there. Those noises had consolidated into a single loud signal when, two months before, he'd sent an advance team to scout locations. He hadn't yet decided who would run the store, though, and that made for lively speculation when his back was turned.

Some said that Greg's eldest cousin, Brad, would be the one; he'd had the Beverly Hills branch for twenty years and knew the West Coast like the back of his hand. Some saw Diandra's Uncle Alex in the post; he'd done well with the Boston store, and San Francisco was like Boston in many respects, so they said. Some fingered Greg's mom, who had guided the Palm Beach branch for nine years and had the kind of quiet class San Francisco demanded.

Not many earmarked Greg for the slot. He was New York through and through, the epitome of the urban bachelor, so even apart from the problem of who would fill his shoes at the New York store if he went west, there was the matter of his seeming love affair with the Big Apple.

Only Diandra knew. She could see it in his eyes each time the subject of San Francisco arose. She could see his hunger. She recognized it because she felt it herself.

She wanted that store, too. She wanted a new challenge in a new city. She'd done what she'd set out to do in Washington, and though she loved the city, there was nothing—and no one—to keep her there.

Knowing that Greg wanted the assignment made her desire it all the more. For years she'd sailed first mate to his captain, earned magna cum laude to his summa, walked in his wake and swallowed water. She'd never again make the mistake of letting him lead her into a labyrinth, but neither had she paid him back for that stunt. She didn't like him. His presence in a room was enough to set her on edge. He'd caused her years of torment on the deepest levels, and if the San Francisco store was to be the great equalizer, she had no problem with that.

Her first thought when she'd received her summons from Old Bart the day before had been that he wanted to talk San Francisco. She'd flown to Palm Beach with her hopes high. But Gregory had been there. His presence had scotched the idea that Bart would hand her the store on a silver platter—either scotched it or boded ill.

Lest her frustration show, she concentrated on greeting Bart, for whom she felt a legitimate fondness. Though slightly short of breath from her dash from the limousine, she was the image of grace and control as she approached the old man with a smile.

Ever the gentleman, despite an eighty-four-year-old body that made physical movement a trial, he stood for her gentle hug.

"I'm sorry to keep you waiting, Bart. The plane was late."

"So Isaac said," Bart replied in the low, gravelly voice that could tear grown men to shreds. Isaac was the chauffeur; he was well-trained to report on delays. "But there wouldn't have been any problem if you'd come in last night, as I'd asked."

"Last night was the Cancer Society benefit at the art museum," she said, knowing that Bart couldn't turn his back on a benefit. "I wanted Casey and York to be represented properly."

"Where's Jordan?" Jordan was Diandra's cousin and, though, twelve years her senior, her second in command.

"With one of our buyers in Rome."

"You have other assistants."

"And they're just that—assistants. I felt I should be there myself. Besides, your invitation was for brunch today. I didn't see the conflict."

"Late planes," Bart grumped.

"I took the earliest flight I could get. I'm sorry." She took a breath that said Enough of that and asked quietly, "How are you, Bart?"

He scowled. "Not bad."

"You're looking well."

"Nah," he said, but his scowl softened. "Hair gets thinner every day, shoulders stoop more, feet shuffle."

"Still, you're looking well." And indeed he was. Inches shorter and pounds lighter than he'd been in his prime, he looked a little like an aging leprechaun—but a handsome one, nonetheless. She plucked at the burgundy handkerchief that peered from the pocket of his navy lounging jacket. "Pretty dapper for an eighty-four-year-old."

"Which isn't saying much, given the competition," Bart grumbled, but there was a hint of mischief in his eyes. "I have to keep up appearances, now, don't I?"

"Sure do," she said, then, in a test of will, forced her smile to remain in place when she turned to Greg. He, too, had risen with her entrance, but though Old Bart's gesture had been one of simple courtesy, Greg's was more complex. He stood to acknowledge her arrival with a show of manners. He also stood, she was convinced, for the sheer intimidation of it.

Gregory York was six foot three inches of well-honed masculinity. His hair, which was on the long side and suggested more than a hint of the rebel, was light brown, shot with gold. His eyes were dark gray and mysterious. The thick but trim beard that he'd worn for years added to that mystery. A shade darker than his hair, it was a barrier between the world and him. It set him apart and made the statement that he was his own man, that his thoughts were private, his emotions no one's affair.

To call the man handsome was to tell only half the story, because even beyond physical details was his manner. Like a lion in a three-piece suit, he exuded power. He was smooth and self-contained. A master of confidence, he knew where he wanted to go and how to get there. He was reasonable unless crossed, but when crossed, he was a terror. What Old Bart did with his voice, Gregory did with his eyes. One look could make strong men pause, weak men stutter, women of all strengths go still and stare.

Diandra had spent years steeling herself against that look, which wasn't to say that she was immune to it, just that she'd had more practice than most. She'd seen it often, not only in CayCorp boardrooms, but at banquets, family outings and on too many other occasions when she'd been haunted by Gregory's presence. He had the ability to stand at the side of a crowd, cross his arms over his chest and command attention without uttering a word. It never failed to infuriate her.

Intimidating was one word for him. *Seductive* was another. Subtle and deceptive, the combination was potent. His purr was as dangerous as his roar.

It was the purr she heard then, as quiet and confident as ever. "How have you been, Diandra?" Taking the hand he offered, he drew her close and kissed her cheek. He always greeted her that way—though he didn't kiss every woman he met. He wasn't the shallow kissy-huggy sort. He was picky. Not that she meant anything to him. He drew her close and kissed her because he knew it disturbed her.

Tamping down that disturbance for reasons of her own pride as well as Old Bart's presence, Diandra looked up to meet Greg's eyes. The firmness in her gaze contradicted the gentleness in her voice. "I've been just fine. And you?"

"Can't complain." He held her back and gave her a deliberate once-over. "You look great."

She returned the once-over. "So do you." He not only looked, but smelled fresh-from-the-shower clean. Ignoring the innate seductive quality in that, she forced herself to focus on his shirt. It was a fine-weave cotton, blue with the thinnest of white stripes at wide intervals—intervals made to look even wider by the breadth of his chest. "Nice shirt. Still shopping at Barney's?"

"Sure," Greg said with a small twist of his lips. It was an old joke. They both knew that the shirt was imported, expensive and sold exclusively in the States at Casey and York. A basic philosophy of the store was that if the people who ran it didn't think its goods either fashionable enough or of high enough quality to wear themselves, something was wrong—and if something was wrong, the blame was easily placed. Since neither Diandra nor Greg cared to take that blame, they took active roles in assuring that Casey and York carried the kinds of clothes they liked to wear. They were, in effect, walking advertisements for their merchandise, which was an extension of the basic philosophy that Old Bart preached.

Greg gave her a second, even more thorough, perusal. She was wearing a chic two-piece silk outfit that was as casual as it was elegant. When his eyes seemed to linger in the vicinity of first her breasts, then her hips, she wanted to scream. She hated men who ogled. She knew he was doing it only to test her patience with Bart looking on. He was baiting her. She was determined not to bite.

"That's next winter's, isn't it?" he asked innocently. The eyes he returned to hers weren't as innocent, nor were the hands that moved lightly on her shoulders.

She ignored both. "It was part of the Milan show two weeks ago." Greg had been in Milan, too, though they'd managed to avoid each other as much as possible. "Delgado's a pushover. Once the show is done, he gives me my pick of samples."

"He adores you."

"He also adores the little boys he has running errands," she said dryly.

"I trust you haven't given him the liberties they have."

She sent him a quelling look.

Undaunted, Greg made a third leisurely perusal of her slender form before dropping his hands. "You should have been a model, you know. You have the body for it."

"Not quite," she said curtly, then took a breath to ease the pique he caused. It helped that he was no longer touching her. His touch was nearly as powerful as his look. "So." She took another breath. "What have you been up to?"

"Not much. And you?"

She shrugged. "I didn't expect to see you here."

"Do tell," he drawled.

"Excuse me?"

His gaze was direct. "I assume you were hoping for a private meeting."

"I wasn't hoping for anything. I got the call that Bart wanted me to come, so I came."

"Without wondering why he'd called?"

"Of course I wondered. Didn't you?"

He didn't have to answer. His eyes said it all; they'd gone charcoal gray, a little faraway and a lot challenging. They had that San Francisco look to them.

And that look had an immediate effect. The competitive beast set butterflies loose in her stomach. "When did you arrive?"

"Last night."

"Things must be slower in New York than Washington."

"No. But I felt it important I be here."

The butterflies began to flutter their wings with greater strength. "Perhaps Bart told you something on the phone that he didn't tell me." She turned an innocent face to Bart, who'd been quietly observing the verbal exchange. "Did I misunderstand? Had you specifically planned something for last night?"

Bart glared at Greg. "No. And you didn't miss a thing. Greg didn't arrive until very late, then slept in this morning. The first time I saw him was twenty minutes ago. If your plane had been on time, he'd have been the one to keep us waiting on brunch." His glare left Greg and was little more than a disgruntled look when it hit Diandra. "I'm hungry." Holding his elbow out to her, he waited until she'd linked her arm through his, then, shuffling his Italian-leather-clad feet over first plush carpet, then polished wood floor, then marble tiles, led the way to the rooftop patio.

As Gregory York stood watching them, he thought of the ironies of life. He'd flown to Palm Beach so sure, *so sure* that Bart had made a decision on the San Francisco store. Of course, Bart had been sleeping when he'd arrived the night before, and he'd been exhausted himself. It had been a long, busy week—a long, busy month—a long, busy year. He vaguely remembered his travel alarm going off, vaguely remembered pushing the button that would set it off again ten minutes later. He must have pushed the wrong button. When he'd finally awoken, he'd bolted from bed and showered and dressed in record time—only to find that Bart was waiting for someone else.

Diandra. Lovely Diandra. Proud, prickly Diandra. Ambitious Diandra.

It was the last that bothered him most. He didn't mind seeing Diandra at corporate meetings or designers' shows or even at the family parties that Old Bart still insisted on throwing. He did mind the idea that she wanted San Francisco.

That store was his. He'd been quietly lobbying for it since before Old Bart had ever realized it was going to be. He'd spent the past ten years working his tail off in New York; he'd earned his stripes. He'd reached the time in his life when he needed a change, and the one he had in mind went beyond locations. He needed a total change of life-style. Regardless of Diandra's schemes, he intended to get it in San Francisco.

Thus determined, he went out onto the patio, where Diandra had just finished helping Bart to his seat. When she turned to her own chair, Greg was there to draw it out for her.

"Thank you," she said politely.

"You're welcome." He took the seat on her left, where the third place was set.

Bart picked up his linen napkin, shook it out and spread it over his lap. He looked from Diandra to Greg and back. "Everything okay?"

"Sure."

"Just fine."

Bart arched a brow and nodded toward the glasses of grapefruit juice that sat in beds of ice before Diandra and Greg. "Drink slowly and appreciate. The citrus crop was lousy this year."

Diandra took a sip. "Then you got the best of it. This is incredibly sweet. Gretchen's still squeezing it fresh?"

"Of course."

She glanced at the dish of prunes that sat at Bart's place in lieu of the juice and said nothing, but her gaze, happening on Greg's, found a ghost of humor there. In that instant, she was hard put not to grin. She didn't like Greg, but they did share a history, and that history included a youthful irreverence for their elders. More times than Diandra could remember, she and Greg—and whichever of their cousins happened to have been around—had snickered about Old Bart's prunes.

Greg cleared his throat and took a healthy drink of his juice.

Diandra busied herself eating the single plump strawberry that rested on the ice as a garnish.

"Just wait," Bart said. "You'll be old before you know it, and then you won't be so smug about what you eat."

"Did we say anything?" Greg asked innocently.

"Bah," Bart scolded. "I know what you were thinking. I'm not dumb or senile. It'd do you good to remember that."

"We do," Diandra said with feeling. "Believe me, we do."

Bart pursed his lips, nodded, then began to eat. Before he'd consumed little more than a third of his prunes, Diandra and Greg were done with their juice. Diandra looked at Greg, who was looking back at her. She glanced away, off toward the patio railing and beyond.

"I always liked the view here," she mused for the sake of harmless conversation, "and it improves with age. There's something hypnotic about the ocean."

"Good thing you don't have an office overlooking it," Greg said. He thought of the office he'd like to have overlooking San Francisco Bay. "You'd be too mesmerized to work."

"You look out on the Statue of Liberty," Diandra returned. "Does she distract you?"

He gave a negligent, one-shouldered shrug. "I don't have the luxury of being distracted. There's too much work to be done."

"That's why," she said in a confident tone, "Manhattan is perfect for you. It doesn't matter if you're surrounded by concrete. You wouldn't be able to take advantage of a view if you had one."

"Would you?"

"Sure." If it were the Golden Gate Bridge, she'd make a point to do it.

"You have that much free time?" he asked skeptically. "I wasn't under the impression we paid our executives to sit staring out windows all day."

"I haven't any more free time than you do."

"You should. Your store isn't as large as mine. If you were working up to capacity, you'd have time on your hands—unless, of course, your capacity is lower."

She sucked in a breath. "What a sexist statement."

"Did I mention sex?"

"You didn't have to."

"It's not a sexist statement," he said. His eyes bored into her. "It's a personal one. You may be doing just fine with the Washington store, but if you think you can handle—"

"Excuse me," Bart broke in, "but I'd like a little peace while I eat."

Greg fell silent. Diandra's eyes flashed him a warning that his own eyes proceeded to defy.

"How *is* everything in New York?" Bart asked him.

Greg stared at Diandra a minute longer before turning his attention to Bart. In the process he fully regained his composure. "I can't complain. The new ad campaign is going over well, if initial sales figures are anything to go by. I'm pleased with Wells-Wescott. The approach they've taken is fresh and aggressive."

Bart turned to Diandra. "What do you think?"

Diandra hadn't rebounded as fully as Greg, but the faint roughness that lingered in her voice passed as earnestness. "I think it's still too early to know anything conclusive. The campaign had to be modified for Washington.''

"It was modified for all of our cities," Greg pointed out.

"I know that," she snapped, "but it was launched in New York, so you have a foot up on us with sales figures." She turned back to Bart and spoke more gently. "It'll be a while yet before we know something concrete."

"Any word-of-mouth feedback?" Bart asked.

"It's good."

Bart looked from one face to the other. "It had better be. There are times when I wake up in the middle of the night having dreamed that the obscene sum we're spending is going straight down the toilet."

"It'll be worth it," Diandra assured him.

"I hope so."

Greg was sure of it. "You have to spend money to make money. You taught us that."

"Oh, yes, but I was teaching you that in the days before inflation took over—and greed. The people at that advertising agency are thieves."

"They're professionals," Diandra said.

Greg added, "We've paid for their expertise. If things pan out the way we expect them to, our profit will pay their fee many times over."

Diandra arched an indulgent brow at Bart. "Does that make us the thieves?"

"Hell, no. People give us their money in exchange for something tangible. They look at whatever they buy, turn it over, wear it, taste it, smell it or whatever, and decide whether they've been gypped. The yard-stick is more visible."

"But we're in this business for a profit, just like Wells-Wescott," Greg pointed out. "So in that sense, we are greedy."

"Speak for yourself," Diandra muttered.

Greg caught the words and refused to let them pass. "I speak for CayCorp. The bottom line is whether or not we make a profit, and if we don't do that, we might as well close shop."

"But there are different ways of making a profit. Nothing we do is underhand. We're not out to rob our customers."

"Of course not. I wasn't the one who mentioned thieves."

She shot a glance skyward. "I was kidding."

"Don't. If we'd been in a restaurant and someone from another table had overheard what you'd said, rumors would have been flying before we'd had dessert."

Diandra tipped up her chin. "I wouldn't know about that. You're the one who's had experience with restaurants and rumors."

During the long moment that Greg was silent, his only movement was the flexing of his jaw. His eyes drilled into hers, hard and sharp. "I assume," he said in a low, dark voice, "that you're referring to the incident last year with Monica Newman."

Working hard to counter the force of that penetrating gaze, Diandra shrugged.

"My lunch with her was solely for the sake of the celebrity telethon."

"That picture of the two of you was pretty condemning."

"That picture," he stated slowly, "was a piece of darkroom wizardry—"

"Which people believed, just the way we hope they'll believe our ad campaign. What kind of opinion do people form about CayCorp when they see one of its executive vice presidents carrying on with a woman who is not only half his age—"

"She isn't half my age. She's twenty."

"She was nineteen then, and married and—"

"Don't say it," he ordered in a deep, deep voice.

"Say what?"

"That she had a fifteen-month-old child whose paternity was in doubt, because that's no concern of mine. I had never met Monica Newman before that day, and I haven't seen her since."

"The papers said otherwise."

"But we know the truth."

"Do we?" she dared, irked by his patronizing tone. "Your reputation hasn't exactly been that of a monk—"

"Diandra," Bart growled. "Please."

But Greg held up a hand. Normally a master of self-control, he was livid. Diandra couldn't have chosen a more inappropriate time to raise something as petty.

"For the record," he said, measuring each word as he stared at her, "the Monica Newman incident was a nonincident. It was forgotten by the press nearly as quickly as it was forgotten by the public, which is what happens to empty stories. You're the only one who seems to remember it. Maybe there's a reason why. A psychological reason. Like jealousy? You love the attention of the press—and if you want to talk reputations, I seem to recall something about a recent issue of *Town Crier* that referred to Diandra Casey as quite the little number around Washington.''

"*Town Crier* is always putting tags on people, very much tongue-in-cheek,'' she answered smoothly.

"Uh-huh.''

"It's true—''

"Oh, please,'' Bart growled. "Keep quiet. Both of you.'' A movement at the door caught his eye and he brightened. "Saved by the cook. I hope you have plenty of food there, Gretchen, because stuffing the mouths of these two may be the only way I'll get any peace.''

Gretchen smiled. She'd been Bart's housekeeper and cook for better than twenty years and had survived where others had failed precisely because she did smile. A certain immunity to tension was a necessity in CayCorp environs.

"Diandra,'' she said with the faintest of brogues, "beautiful as ever.''

Taking a deep, calming breath, Diandra smiled. She'd always liked Gretchen. "And you are a sight for sore eyes. What have you got there?''

Gretchen set the tray on the edge of the table and began to transfer plates. "I have scrambled eggs, Canadian bacon, apricot-filled croissants and date-nut muffins.''

Diandra, minus her smile, looked at Greg. "Will that be enough to fill your mouth?''

Before he could answer, Gretchen was talking again. "I do not have the fried potatoes you like so much, Gregory. Mr. Bart wouldn't let me make them. He said they'd be too great a temptation for him. He's not supposed to eat them.''

Greg was thinking that he wasn't, either, but he had no intention of opening that particular can of worms to either Bart's rumination or Diandra's pontification. "No harm.'' He patted his stomach. "We're all probably just as well without them.'' He lowered his voice and leaned closer to Gretchen. "Maybe another time you'll make up a batch and we'll pig out in the kitchen, just you and me. Deal?''

Gretchen's smile grew nearly as broad as her girth. "Deal.'' Having emptied her tray, she began to pour coffee while the three at the table helped themselves to the food she'd prepared. When she left, the only sound that remained was the soft click of utensils.

Conjuring up a blinder on her left side, Diandra did her best to ignore Gregory. It wasn't as difficult as it might have been, since Bart was the one who, at that moment, gave her pause. He seemed perfectly at ease and undisturbed, so much so that it was nerve-racking. Bart didn't do things without cause. He had summoned her to Palm Beach. She wanted to know why.

So did Greg. From the time he'd been five, when his grandfather had sat him down, given him a tiny spiral-bound notebook and taught him to keep a written tally of the money he had and the money he spent, he'd known Bart as a businessman. Business always came first. Even Bart's wife, Emma, had understood that. Bart never wasted time. He wasn't the kind of man who invited two of the corporation's vice presidents to brunch and then sat around discussing grapefruit.

Greg wondered if Bart's age was catching up to him. The physical slowdown was obvious and not new. Nor was the occasional lapse of memory with regard to a name or word. But otherwise Bart had remained sharp. Today, though, there seemed a softening to that sharpness. It made Greg uneasy.

Between his eggs and a muffin, Bart put down his fork. "Tell me," he said to Diandra. "How is young Marshall working out?"

Young Marshall was Diandra's cousin, twenty-two and fresh from school. Diandra exchanged an uncomfortable glance with Greg before answering. "I'm not sure. I sent him to St. Louis."

Bart blinked. "You did what?"

"Sent him to St. Louis. Thomas seemed the logical one to train him."

"Why wasn't I consulted?"

"Because it all happened last month, and you were in Hong Kong at the time."

"Why wasn't I notified when I got back?"

"Because it was settled," Diandra said quietly.

"But I wanted him in Washington."

"As I understood it," she corrected chidingly, "you wanted him in New York." She sliced a look to her left. "Greg foisted him on me."

Bart pursed his lips. "Greg's arguments were sound. The boy was lost in New York."

"Well, he wasn't lost in Washington. It was more the other way around. From the minute he arrived, he imagined himself the savior of every female page in the Senate. He was totally obnoxious." Catching herself, she tried to sound more professional. "Beyond that, there were problems at work."

"What kind of problems?" Bart demanded.

"He had," Greg joined the discussion to intone, "delusions of grandeur."

Diandra couldn't have put it better herself. "He thought himself above being a stock boy, but that's how we all began. Start at the bottom and know the business, you always said. We were working summers when we were in high school, so by the time we were in college we had already climbed some. Marshall didn't work summers when he was in high school."

"He said he didn't need the money," Greg interjected. "Neither did we, but still we worked. There was pride involved. He lacks it."

"He spent most of his college summers traveling," Diandra went on, "so suddenly he found himself with a college degree and no work experience. He expected to join the company as a junior-level executive, but he doesn't know the first thing about business. He argues that he's family and that he should be on par with the other cousins, but nearly all of us have graduate degrees.'' She paused for a breath. "I've worked hard to get where I am. He wants it for nothing.''

"He's a nice kid, Bart, just a little spoiled.''

"A *lot* spoiled,'' Diandra corrected.

Greg shot her an annoyed look before continuing. "He needs to have limits set. We sent him to St. Louis because Thomas runs a rigid bureaucracy. The kid isn't a total loss. He has potential.''

"That's *your* opinion.''

"Well, it's worth something,'' Greg argued. "I've seen lots of employees come and go, and the best have spunk. Marshall has that. It just needs to be channeled.''

"But he hates the work!''

"So did I. I hated the stockroom, and I wasn't madly in love with selling shoes, either. There were times during those first few years when I seriously considered being an accountant.''

"You should have been one.''

"I was lousy with figures.''

"Tell that to the teeny-boppers,'' she muttered.

Greg glared. "What is that supposed to mean?''

"Stop!'' Bart broke in gruffly. "What *is* it with you two?''

Both heads swung his way, both faces registering surprise, as though they'd momentarily forgotten he was there. Then they exchanged glances—a little annoyed, a little dismayed, even a little apprehensive. They jumped when Bart slapped both palms on the tabletop.

"I did not bring you here to discuss San Francisco."

Diandra's mouth felt suddenly dry. She didn't dare betray her guilt by looking at Greg, and she knew he wouldn't look at her. His expression would be smooth, confident. It wouldn't reveal a thing.

"I haven't made a decision on that," Bart went on, "and frankly, I'm not pleased with what I see here."

Diandra took a breath. "Gregory and I rub each other the wrong way—"

"But that has nothing to do with professional qualifications," Greg finished.

"But *why* do you rub each other the wrong way?" Bart asked.

"He's impossibly arrogant—"

"She's incredibly self-centered—"

Diandra gawked at Greg. "Self-centered? What have I ever done to you—"

"If I'm arrogant," Greg barked, "I've earned the right—"

"That's *enough*," Bart said. He sat back in his chair and glared at them, his wrinkled brow all but meeting his eyes. Then he dropped his gaze to his lap. He pressed his lips together. Methodically he folded his napkin and put it beside his plate.

Diandra waited then, waited for that second shoe to fall. Bart had called them to Palm Beach for some reason, and he claimed it wasn't to talk about the San Francisco store. She held her breath in anticipation, as did Greg.

"I called the two of you here," Bart began in a voice that was low and oddly sad, "because I need your help." Slowly he raised his eyes and focused first on Greg, then Diandra. "I'm selling the Boston town house. Its contents have to be sorted through, cataloged and crated." His gaze linked them. "I want you to do it."

2

Unsure that she'd heard right, Diandra stared at Bart. When she shifted a perplexed glance to Greg, she found him looking just as confused.

"You're selling the town house?" he asked in a strangely uncertain voice.

Bart nodded.

Diandra leaned forward. "But why?"

"Because I spend most of my time here, and when I'm not here, I'm at business meetings somewhere else. Since we moved our corporate headquarters to New York, I've had even less call to be in Boston. I only get there once or twice a year now. The town house is going to waste."

"But it's part of the family," Diandra argued, using the term "family" loosely but comfortably. As a Casey, she'd spent as much time in that Beacon Hill home as many a York had. "You've owned it for... how many years?"

"Sixty," Greg supplied. "He bought it when he and Emma were first married." He faced Bart. "That's a lot of history to cut off, just like that. There must be someone in the family who wants it."

"Do you?" Bart asked him.

Greg drew his head back at the sudden question. "Sure I do, but I live in New York. I wouldn't use it any more than you. Besides," he added with a wry twist of his lips, "I can't afford two homes. You don't pay me enough."

"Like hell I don't," Bart mumbled as his gaze swung to Diandra. "How about you?"

"I'd take it in a minute, but I'm in Washington. Even aside from the issue of money, I don't have the time to do the place justice." She gave a helpless frown. "There must be another one of us who would."

"Tell me who," Bart ordered. "I've been trying to find the right someone for months. My children either have their own homes or are dead. My grandchildren either have their own homes or don't deserve them. I've been through the list, including your side, Diandra, and the only one remotely in a position to take over the town house, since he has the Boston store, is your Uncle Alex, but, frankly, I'd rather sell it to Lassie."

Diandra knew enough to keep still. Uncle Alex was her late mother's twin brother, and despite the obvious sex difference, the physical resemblance between them had been marked. Unfortunately Bart hadn't thought well of Diandra's mother at the time of her death, and though he treated Alex with professional respect, there was no love lost between them. When Bart looked at Alex, he saw Abby, and when that happened, Bart was reminded that his favored son, Greg's father, was also dead. It was understandable that for purely emotional reasons Bart wouldn't want Alex taking over the town house.

"So," Bart went on, "there's no one. I've already had an offer on the place and if I accept it, it'll have to be emptied."

"You've had an offer?" Diandra echoed in dismay. "How long has it been on the market?"

"It hasn't officially been listed. But I've been talking with my broker for several weeks, and out of the blue she came up with an offer. The fellow who wants it is an executive who's being transferred to Boston. He's willing to pay top dollar, but he wants to get in soon. I'll be making a decision today."

"You sound as though you've already made it," Greg observed.

Bart didn't answer.

Leaning back in his chair, Greg buried his hands in the pockets of his slacks. He was surprised at how bothered he was by the idea of Bart's selling the town house. He'd never thought himself the sentimental sort, but he felt an affinity for the house. If only it were in San Francisco.

But it wasn't, and there was Bart's request to be considered. "Emptied. Okay. Exactly what does that entail?"

"Going through the place room by room. Listing the contents of each room. Disposing of everything in an appropriate fashion. Some things should be shipped to me, some sold, some donated to museums or charity, some tossed out."

"And you want us—" Diandra waggled a skeptical finger between herself and Greg "—to do that?"

Bart nodded.

Greg cleared his throat. He might have laughed—the proposal was that ludicrous—but one didn't laugh at Bartholomew York. One reasoned in a very quiet, very sane manner. "Do you have any idea how long a project like that would take?"

"As I see it—" Bart squinted one eye "—a week—two at the most." He opened both eyes. "If you go at it conscientiously, that is."

"You have to be kidding," Diandra said.

"I'm not."

She eyed him askance. "You're serious?"

"Very."

She raised both brows. "Two weeks?"

"One, if you're quick."

"But that's absurd!" she argued, momentarily throwing caution to the winds. "I don't know about Greg, but I can't take a week off from work. Forget two. That'd be a total pipe dream."

Outwardly calm, Greg came forward and linked his fingers at the top of his plate. Only someone who was aware of the smallest details would have noticed that his knuckles were white. "When had you intended to have this done?"

"Next week."

"Next week!" Diandra cried. "Bart, that's impossible!"

"Nothing's impossible."

"Easy for you to say. Have you any idea what's on my calendar for next week?"

Bart gave a small self-satisfied smile. "I know exactly what's on your calendar for next week. You have an assortment of management and sales meetings. You have a conference scheduled with Peter Walsh and his underlings to discuss a reorganization in gourmet foods. You have a meeting about the Christmas catalog. You have appointments with three potential replacements for Nancy Soo, who headed the personnel department for four years, has been on maternity leave for three months and now finds that she wants to play mother full-time. You have—" He paused, arched a sparse gray brow. "Shall I go on?"

She shook her head. "You've checked with my secretary. You know how fully booked next week is."

He flicked a gnarled hand at the insignificance of the problem. "There's nothing on your schedule that can't be either postponed or handled by someone else."

She stared. "Cleaning out the town house takes precedence over the running of a multimillion-dollar business?"

"In this case, yes."

"But *anyone* can clean out the town house."

His smile faded. "That's where you're wrong. It's not just a matter of cleaning. It's a matter of sorting through materials that have been collected over a period of more than half a century. For that I need someone who cares. I'd do it if I could, but I don't have the physical wherewithal. You have the strength.

You also have the emotional involvement. And I trust you—both of you—which is more than I can say for most."

Both of you. Diandra looked at Greg. He held her gaze for a minute, then pushed back his chair, stood and crossed the patio to stand at the railing looking out to sea. She watched his tall form, saw the tension in his shoulders and knew he had to be thinking her thoughts.

She was right. He was thinking about the week that lay ahead of him in New York, thinking that the last thing he could afford to do was to cancel meetings, shift conferences, postpone interviews. Putting things off now would only jam-pack his schedule down the road, and the road ahead was busy enough. For just that reason, it had been years since he'd taken a bona fide vacation. Bart knew that.

Thrusting a hand through the thickness of his hair, he left that hand at the back of his head while he flexed the muscles of his shoulders. Tension settled there first; it always had. He swam to counter it, played tennis to expend even more nervous energy— for whatever good either activity did. When he chased the tension from his shoulders, it settled in his stomach. He really did need a break.

But at Bart's town house in Boston? With *Diandra*?

That was probably the worst part. It was bad enough that Bart was asking him to take a week off from work in New York, but thinking of spending that week with Diandra was like watching a storm approach across a lake. He and she were misaligned gears; two minutes together, rubbing each other the wrong way, and sparks flew.

He could just see it. They'd be at each other's throat in no time. Didn't Bart know that?

His hand fell to the back of his neck and began to rub the tight muscles there as he listened to Diandra's voice at the table.

"But why this week?" she asked. "If we had some advance notice, we'd have an easier time making arrangements."

"This week because it may take you *two* weeks, and that will take us right up to the time when my buyer wants to take title."

"Put him off a little."

"There's no reason why I should."

She offered it. "An extra week or two would make things easier for Greg and me."

Bart ignored that. "None of us is using the house. He wants it cleared so that he can pass papers and get his decorators in there."

"He's asking a lot."

"He's paying a lot."

When she fell quiet, Greg allowed a wry smile. Apparently she didn't know the futility of arguing. Bart had his mind made up. That message came across in every sentence he spoke. He'd invited them to Palm Beach not to ask but to inform them that they'd be spending their next week in Boston, and the more she argued, the more he'd dig in his heels. But she was a rebellious creature. She refused to accept that someone else could control her. She was willful to the core—just as her mother had been. But he wasn't his father. He wasn't about to be brought down by Diandra Casey—any more than he was about to spend a week in close quarters with her.

He was about to offer to do the house himself when Diandra came up with her own suggestion. "Would it be possible," she began with cautious optimism, "for Greg and I to take shifts? I could work at the town house for several days, then return to Washington while he took over in Boston." She glanced up when Greg turned around, but quickly returned her attention to Bart. "After several more days, I'd relieve him, so he could go back to New York. That way neither of us would have such a solid stretch away from the office."

But Bart was shaking his head. "The most time-effective method is to have the two of you working together for as long as it takes."

Diandra wasn't giving up. "What if I brought an assistant with me from Washington? I'm sure Greg has someone he could bring. That way there'd always be two people working here."

"I don't want strangers in my house. I want you and Greg."

"I'd bring Jordan. Greg could bring Ben. They're not strangers, they're family."

Bart grunted. "If I didn't know better, Diandra, I'd think that you were frightened of spending a week with Greg."

Leaning back against the rail, Greg folded his arms over his chest and waited with interest for Diandra's response. It came very quickly and, to his satisfaction, with a crimson flush.

"Me? Frightened of him? That's absurd!"

"Then it must be that you're frightened of a little hard work, and if that's the case, I don't see how I can possibly consider you for San Francisco."

Diandra sucked in a sharp breath. Her gaze darted from Bart to Greg and back, and even Greg could see the hurt there. "Low blow, Bart," she whispered. "I don't deserve that."

"Maybe not," Bart relented to a point, "but neither do I deserve this grief. If I had my druthers, I wouldn't be giving up the town house. If I had my druthers, I wouldn't be eighty-four years old." His expression softened, saddened. "But I don't have my druthers. I haven't many more years left, and I want the town house taken care of before I'm gone. It holds special memories for me. I'm entrusting you with their care."

Diandra was deeply touched, but before she could respond, he went on.

"I've paid my dues in life. I think it's time I called in a few IOUs." He paused. "I've been generous over the years, haven't I?"

His words brought an ache to her chest. She knew that he wasn't talking of money, or even of power, but of his feelings toward her mother. Another man might have taken those feelings out on Diandra. Bart hadn't.

"You've been more than generous," she conceded softly.

Pressing his thin lips together, Bart gave a half nod. "Then I'm asking for one week of your time in return. Will you give it?"

"Of course."

Bart swiveled his eyes toward Greg. "And you?"

Knowing that he had no other choice, given what Bart had just done to Diandra, Greg nodded. A storm might be coming across the lake, but he'd faced storms before and survived. He'd do it this time, too.

The brunch in Palm Beach had been on Saturday. Later that day, Diandra flew back to Washington, Greg to New York, each with feelings of impending doom. Those feelings only intensified as the weekend passed, and by the time Monday morning arrived, both Greg's staff in New York and Diandra's in Washington were suffering the ill humor of their respective bosses.

Diandra had it worse than Greg. Thanks to the arrangements Bart had made even before her Palm Beach visit, she was to be picked up first. His private plane was to take off from Washington in midafternoon on Monday, go north to pick up Greg, then fly on to Boston. That gave her only part of Monday to reorganize a full week's worth of business—she couldn't even *think* what would happen if closing up the town house took longer than that. As it was, she'd called her secretary in to work on Sunday afternoon, had stayed at the office until past eleven that night, then met her there again at seven the next morning. By the time her staff arrived, she had lengthy lists of what was to be done in her absence and by whom. Unfortunately she ran a tight ship anyway, which meant that none of her top-level people sat twiddling their thumbs. Their schedules were nearly as busy as hers, a fact they reminded her of repeatedly as they ran in and out of her office that morning.

She was feeling totally besieged when the time came for her to leave for the airport. Grabbing the small bag that contained the few necessities she figured she'd need for the week, she dashed from her office with little more than a quick wave and collapsed wearily in the back of the limousine that waited outside. An hour later, she was in Bart's jet en route to New York.

Greg popped an antacid into his mouth as his long strides ate up the stretch of tarmac between his limo and Bart's plane. He supposed he looked as composed as ever; that was part of the image. On the inside, though, he felt ragged. In essence, he had condensed five working days into one—actually two since he'd spent most of Sunday in the office—and he was feeling the backlash.

When he'd been twenty-five, even thirty, he'd thrived on crises. Even when it seemed the world was going to hell in a bucket, he'd been able to come through calmly, coolly and constructively. He could still come through that way, but now he paid more of a price.

Somewhere it had to end, he knew. He had to find a compromise between his present hectic life and the more placid one his doctor recommended. He was pinning his hopes on San Francisco. If he got the assignment, he'd do things differently. He'd establish more regular hours, for one thing. For another, he'd delegate authority more. His shoulders were broad, but not broad enough to bear the weight they had. He was tired. It was as simple as that.

With a grimace, he took the last step and swung into the plane. He was greeted by the copilot, who immediately drew up the steps, closed the door and took his place in the cockpit with the pilot.

Tossing his duffel bag into the luggage bin, Greg turned toward the cabin. It was a single large compartment with a combination bar/kitchenette at one end and an assortment of upholstered furniture anchored at the other. Diandra was in one of the executive lounge chairs, her head against its back, her hands on each arm, her legs crossed gracefully at the knee. She wore a lightweight wool suit—pleated skirt, oversize blazer, silk blouse—and had clearly come straight from the office. The way she was staring at him suggested she was as disgusted with the situation as he was.

Lowering himself into a chair that matched hers, he buckled his seat belt, put his elbow on the arm of the chair and his jaw on his fist and stared right back at her.

Neither of them spoke as the plane taxied down the runway, waited a brief time for clearance, then took off. Nor did they speak as they gained altitude and headed northeast.

Diandra didn't trust herself to say a thing. She was too annoyed to say anything nice, and saying something sarcastic would only invite retribution. She wasn't up for retribution. The past two days had been the pits. She was too tired to spar with Greg.

That put her at a disadvantage—and one more disadvantage she didn't need. As it was, the cabin seemed to have shrunk with Greg's arrival. He was a large man—lean but large—and the way his eyes pierced her made her heart thud. It was always that way. She could tell the moment he entered a room. Her skin would begin to prickle, her pulse to race. She'd long since stopped fighting it, had simply accepted that she was viscerally attuned to him.

He was her past, and he unsettled her. When she was unsettled, she tended to be less in control, and when she was less in control, she was less prudent. That was what had happened during brunch with Bart. She'd been trading barbs with Greg, which had unsettled her, so that even after he'd withdrawn from the fray, she'd run on at the mouth to Bart. While Greg had stood silently to the side—listening, letting her ask the questions he was, no doubt, wondering about himself—she'd nearly dug herself into a hole.

If only he'd spoken up. But he'd stood there, silent, while she'd argued. If he'd said no to Boston, she might have been able to do it, too. But he hadn't said no. He hadn't said a thing until Bart had softened her into saying yes—and once she'd done that, Greg had been locked in as well. He wasn't about to give her an edge on the San Francisco store, any more than she'd have given him one. She felt as though she were being held up for ransom and had no choice but to pay.

On the plus side, it looked as though she and Greg were the two remaining finalists for the post. Bart wasn't a manipulative man when it came to business; he was too blunt for that. If he were leaning toward someone else, he'd have said so instead of insisting that she and Greg handle the Beacon Hill town house because he "trusted" them.

Having come this far, she couldn't afford to antagonize Bart. Neither could Greg, which was why, she knew, he'd agreed to come. Unfortunately once they reached the town house they'd be on their own. Bart wouldn't be there to serve as a tempering force. She feared things were going to get hairy before the week was out.

Greg was thinking much the same thing but wondering at the same time how a woman who looked as harmless could be so lethal. She really was lovely; he had to grant her that. Her skin was an ivory hue, smooth and dewy. Her eyes were dark brown and large, her nose small and straight, her lips delicately defined. She wore makeup skillfully, if sparingly, using color to highlight rather than exaggerate. Her hair was raven black and lustrous, and she wore it straight, cut to just below the chin in a modern pageboy. The bangs that covered her forehead only added to the fragile look of her face—again a deception, he mused.

She was a businesswoman through and through, about as fragile as a steel girder.

The plane reached its cruising altitude and leveled off, and still they regarded each other in silence. Diandra felt as if she were being dissected with a dull and rusty knife, though how much of that internal scraping was due to residual tension from the office, she didn't know. She did know, with each minute she held Greg's gaze, that she was exhausted. Making a small sound of disgust, she turned her head aside and closed her eyes.

"Something wrong?" Greg asked in a voice that was low and smooth.

The short question—and its underlying sarcasm— set her off. Without opening her eyes, she said, "Your hair's too long, do you know that? You look like a throwback to the sixties."

"Is that so?"

"Yes."

"I don't dress like one."

"You don't dare dress like one, or you'll be out of a job." She pictured the way he was dressed. Straight-from-the-office neat, he was wearing a dark three-piece suit. It was British, obviously hand cut and so conservative as to be mod—at least on him. He had the vest unbuttoned, which added to the rakish look of his hair and beard. Yes, rakish. Annoyingly so. "I'm surprised no one else has complained."

"About my hair? It hasn't hurt business."

"What kind of executive wears his hair long and shaggy?" It wasn't actually shaggy—he had it professionally styled—but still it brushed his collar at the back.

"The kind who thinks for himself," he answered without pause. "The successful kind."

She gave an unladylike snort but lapsed into silence. He always had a retort. She couldn't win, and if she couldn't win, there wasn't much point in playing the game.

Greg had other ideas. "And you're a fine one to mention my image, when you look like you're on your last leg." He felt as if he was on his, which, he supposed, was one reason that he was striking back. Normally he'd rise above the situation and remain still, but he was feeling testy. Even when he was at his best, Diandra could get to him where others couldn't, and he was far from his best just then.

"I'm tired," she said, opening her eyes to meet his. "I worked nearly round the clock to free things up so I could do this, and it's all your fault."

"*My* fault."

"You're a coward."

Greg didn't mind comments about his hair. He felt comfortable with his appearance, confident that he always looked clean and well-groomed. But attacks on his character were something else. Any smug, indulgent tone that had been in his voice vanished. "I think you ought to explain that."

"With pleasure. If you had spoken up in Palm Beach, neither of us would be here. It would have been two against one, us against Bart. We might have been able to convince him either not to sell the town house or to delay the sale for a while. What's his rush, anyway? He's owned the place for sixty years, what difference would a few more months make?''

"He has a buyer."

"So if that one fizzled, he'd get another. The town house is prime Beacon Hill property. He hadn't even officially listed the place, and it sold. Just think of what might have happened if he'd waited. *Five* people would have wanted it, there'd have been a bidding war, and Bart would have come away even richer."

"He doesn't need the money," Greg pointed out.

"Still, why the rush? It doesn't make sense."

Speaking very slowly and with disdain, Greg said, "Hasn't it occurred to you that he's feeling pain? He said that if he had his choice he wouldn't be selling. He may be afraid that if he waits, he'll chicken out. So he's looking to make a quick, clean break."

"But why us? I can name several others who could do the job."

"He trusts us."

"You and me—you *and* me? He knows we don't get along!"

"Oh? Now how does he know that?"

"He heard us bickering, for one thing."

"But that was on Saturday, after he'd made his plans. Has he ever seen us bickering before?"

Diandra thought about that and realized Greg was right. Bart had probably never seen them bicker before, and with good reason.

Greg spelled it out in a low, sure voice. "We see each other as little as possible. Family occasions, board meetings, conferences—maybe once or twice a month we're in the same room, but there are always other people around. One of us may express a view that conflicts with the other's, but there are usually a third and a fourth conflicting view, too. We've never had to work together, really work together. We've never tackled each other head-on. So how was Bart to know we're like fire and water?''

"Now who's underestimating him?" Diandra lashed back. "He knew, Greg. He had to know. There's no *way* we could get along, given what happened with my mother and your father."

Her words hung in the air, then left a resounding silence that not even the steady drone of the jet engines could break.

Greg didn't move an inch; every one of his muscles was taut. Diandra's remark had immediately focused his mind on the two gravestones that stood side by side in the old island cemetery off the coast of Maine. Sixteen years they'd been gone, and still it hurt. It would always hurt, because just as the bodies had never been found amid the airplane debris in the ocean, answers had never been found, either. Nor would they be, it seemed. The two people who could explain why they'd done what they had were gone.

And Diandra's basic question remained. Why had Bart thrust her and Greg together?

The corner of Greg's mouth curled in a mirthless expression. "Maybe my grandfather has developed a warped sense of humor in his old age. He knows we both want San Francisco. He can't make the decision himself. So he's throwing us into the ring to slug it out. The one who emerges at the end of the week intact is the one who goes west.''

''That's sick.''

Greg shrugged. ''Then again, maybe it's a simple test of loyalty. He wants to know how far we'll go for him. As people get older, they sometimes need that kind of reassurance—like the child who needs a special hug every so often.''

''Ah, we're into psychology now.''

Ignoring the barb, he stared her down. ''My mother's going through something like that.''

Diandra had always thought of Greg's mother as a totally together woman—no, she corrected herself, that had only been true in the last nine or ten years. Before that, Sophia had been a woman without a cause, and before that—before her husband had died—she'd been little more than a shadow.

Diandra wanted to ask more, but Greg's look didn't invite questions. He blamed her mother for his mother's woes, and she was her mother's daughter. Greg wasn't as generous as Bart.

The whole mess was painful for Diandra, too. So she closed her eyes and turned her head away again. In the minutes of silence that followed, the pain faded. A new pain arose when, out of nowhere, Greg asked, ''Hot weekend?''

Her eyes popped back open. ''What?''

''Who's keeping you awake at night these days?''

''Work is keeping me awake. I told you that.''

Greg crossed his long legs. "Last I heard, you were dating a Senatorial aide from Wyoming, but that was more than a month ago. I assume it's over and you've moved on."

Diandra pressed her lips together and said nothing.

"Before that," Greg continued in a low, goading voice, "it was a lawyer from the Department of Justice. At least that's what the grapevine said."

"What grapevine?"

"The CayCorp one, comprising all sorts of aunts, uncles and cousins. Jealousy is rampant, Diandra. You've come a long way in a short time. The backstabbers are having a field day."

"And you're out there cheering them on?"

He shook his head. "Not my style. But I do hear what they say, and the word is that you're a siren."

You're a siren, Abby. Stay away from him.

Diandra lost some of her color. "Backstabbers are backstabbers. Their word isn't worth much."

"Still, they offer food for thought. So who's your latest catch? Someone with the Department of Defense? Or the Swedish embassy?"

"You're being unfair."

"I'm as curious as the next guy."

"My personal life is none of your business."

His features tightened. "Not so. We'll be together for the next week, you and me. I think I ought to know what's what." He made a slow perusal of her figure, and when his eyes returned to hers they were dark, oddly sensual. "Are there going to be late-night calls from a lover? Secret trysts in the park?"

That call you got late last night wasn't from your good friend Donna, and you didn't go to her house to talk her out of a binge. You ran out to see him, *didn't you?*

Diandra felt a twinge of nausea. Slumping in the chair, she closed her eyes and took a deep breath.

"What's wrong, Diandra?" came Greg's quiet voice. "Have I hit a raw spot?"

"I don't believe you'd know a raw spot if it hit you in the face," she said in a weary voice. "You have to be one of the most insensitive men I've ever met." She opened her eyes. "But then, the apple doesn't fall far from the tree, does it?"

Greg stared at her hard. So she thought him insensitive? So she thought his *father* insensitive? That only proved how little she knew.

But of course she was Abby's daughter. What else could she say? She was Abby's daughter and a social butterfly just as her mother had been. Granted, Diandra had a demanding career, but that didn't mean she couldn't flit around during off hours.

Beautiful women were often that way, Greg had decided. Once they learned the power of their beauty, they played on it. Abby had done that. She'd enchanted men with the toss of her hair, the sway of her hips, the smallest of smiles. Some argued that she'd been bored with her life, but Greg couldn't buy that. She'd had a husband and a daughter, and if she'd wanted to work, she could have taken her pick of positions in the business. She'd turned all that down to spend her days plotting her nights, when she'd be in the arms of her husband's best friend.

Unbuckling his seat belt, Greg went to the bar, poured himself a shot of Scotch and tossed it back. Setting the glass down, he turned to lean against the bar.

Diandra hadn't moved. She was watching him, looking a little cornered, he thought. But beautiful, ah, yes, beautiful. Even exhausted, she had a certain aura, a promise of future fire. He could understand why men would flock to her. He bet she'd be dynamite in bed.

"We're starting our approach into Logan, Mr. York," the copilot appeared at the door of the cabin to say.

Returning to his chair, Greg buckled himself in.

He bet she'd be dynamite in bed.

He looked at Diandra. Her head was downcast, forehead resting on two fingertips. Her hair was a glossy black veil around her face, closing it from his view, but if she thought to tempt him with the pose, she had much to learn about his tastes. He liked his women open and honest.

He bet she'd be dynamite in bed.

She was tall, slender but shapely, with curves in all the right spots. She had the body of a California blonde, the temper of a redhead and the allure of a brunette, yet her hair was midnight black. A bundle of contradictions? No. Greg had her figured out. She was self-centered and aggressive, effective in business because she was bright and driven. On a personal level, she was trouble. Still . . .

He bet she'd be dynamite in bed.

The plane soared low over the harbor and touched down onto the runway with a small bump. The faint jarring was enough to bring Greg to his senses. Diandra might be dynamite in bed, but he'd never know for a fact, because he had no intention of joining her there.

She could lure other sailors to the rocks, but not him. He was deaf to her song.

Frederick, Bart's chauffeur, butler, spare cook and handyman, was waiting with the car near the executive hangar when the jet taxied up. He greeted Diandra and Greg with the formal nod that was his style, took their bags from the copilot and stowed them in the trunk of the large Mercedes.

"Will there be more?" he asked, eyeing the roomy trunk.

"That's it," Greg said.

Diandra was already heading for the car door. "No more."

Greg followed her into the back seat of the roomy sedan. "No more? That little bag couldn't hold much more than a blow dryer, a makeup case and a handful of sexy nighties. Of course, that may be all you'll need."

"All I'll need," she said, slicing him a sharp glance, "is my oldest shirts and jeans, and that's exactly what I brought."

Frederick started the car and pulled away from the hangar.

"No sexy nighties?" Greg asked in a suggestively deep voice.

"Not quite."

"What do you sleep in?"

She looked out the window. Dusk had fallen, blurring details of the terminals they passed. They might have been in any of a dozen airports in any of a dozen cities. She wished she were anywhere but here.

"Diandra?"

"Does it matter?"

"Yes, it matters. If it's going to be just you and me running around in the halls at night, I should know what to expect."

"Ask Frederick what he wears to bed."

"We won't be near Frederick. He has his own apartment in the basement. So what is it, Diandra? I'd have guessed sexy nighties or nothing, and since you've nixed sexy nighties, that leaves nothing."

"Suit yourself."

"I intend to."

Gritting her teeth, she concentrated on the scene beyond the window. But there was nothing terribly exciting about rush-hour traffic, and when the Mercedes finally paid its toll and entered the tunnel, she felt as though the world had closed in. In sheer desperation—hearing Greg's voice was better than not hearing it and wondering what he was thinking—she blurted out, "What in the devil does that mean—you intend to suit yourself?"

"It means," he said in a menacingly low voice, "that I'm the senior member of this little operation, therefore I'm the one in command. If you want to play while you're here, you'll do it on your own time and somewhere else."

"I don't believe you," she murmured to the window. Traffic was stop and go in the tunnel. She looked at the tiles that lined the walls and wondered, as she had so many times before, what would happen if there were a leak and the harbor started pouring in. Just then, one part of her would have welcomed the diversion.

"Senior member," she muttered, then dropped her voice and mimicked, "I'm the one in command." The sputtering noise she made told her opinion of that, but it wasn't enough. "That's how trouble starts, when big men who think they know everything take command." She turned to him. His face had the eerie gray cast that came from the reflection of light in the tunnel, but his eyes were as dark and, yes, commanding as ever. Steeling herself against their force, she said, "I don't recall Bart saying anything about senior members. As far as I'm concerned, you can handle one room, I'll handle another. The less our paths cross the better."

"You're going to pack cartons, lift them, stack them?"

"I'm not a weakling."

"You're a woman."

"For *heaven*'s sake."

"It's a biological fact. You have less muscle than I do."

"So I'll pack cartons, then leave them for you to lift and stack. Sound fair?"

"Sounds like I'm being used."

"Then you worry about your work, I'll worry about mine." She felt an invisible vise loosen as they left the tunnel and skirted the north end. Instinctively she turned her head for a look down Hanover Street. As always, people milled outside the shops and homes that lined the narrow street. There was a warmth to the Italian district that had always appealed to her. For the first time since she'd learned she was coming north, she felt a glimmer of affection for Boston.

Sitting back in her seat again, she watched the buildings of Government Center go by. Ahead was the climb up Beacon Hill, then the short descent to Bart's street. For a brief minute, she was comfortable, relaxing on the wave of a sense of homecoming. Then Greg's voice broke into her thoughts, and all comfort vanished.

"Pull over at the pharmacy, Frederick. I want to run in for something."

Diandra stared at his stony features. "The pharmacy," she stated slowly, "is only two blocks from the town house. The considerate thing to do would be to let us go to the town house first, then run to the drugstore yourself."

"I never claimed to be considerate," Greg said. He was out the door the minute the car reached the curb.

Diandra watched him go, saw him disappear into the store, then reappear moments later popping something into his mouth. He hadn't held them up for long, but she was in no mood to be indulgent.

"And you think I'm taking orders from you?" she burst out. "Think again, bud."

He swallowed whatever he'd chewed and said nothing.

Frederick drove on.

She threw a hand in the air. "I don't know why I'm surprised. Your family specializes in taking command."

"It's the secret of our success," he said, staring straight ahead.

"Right. You thrive on controlling. Manipulating. Using."

He arched a brow. "Are you talking about me?"

"If the shoe fits . . ."

"It doesn't."

"Is that a fact?"

"Yes."

"Then I must be confusing you with another Gregory York."

Greg felt the antacid tablet he'd just chewed do an about-face in his gullet. He swallowed hard and said tightly, "My father's dead. Leave him be."

Diandra didn't respond. She was too busy trying to control her annoyance. Or was it panic? The town house had come into view, Frederick was slowing the car to make the turn into the drive, she felt as if she were trapped.

But the longer she remained silent, the more Greg needed to speak. She'd made specific accusations, and since his father wasn't there to defend himself, the job fell to Greg. "My father was neither a manipulator nor a user. His sole mistake was in falling for your mother. If anyone was the user in that relationship, she was."

Frederick guided the car down the brick-enclosed driveway and into the open courtyard.

"That's insane," Diandra muttered.

"I don't think so."

"How could my mother have possibly used your father? What did he have that she wanted—that her own husband couldn't give her?" The car had come to a halt. She tugged open the door and slid out, leaving the question rhetorical.

Greg wasn't satisfied with that. Following her out of the car and toward the house, he said, "My dad had strength. He was an exciting man. Of him and John, he was by far the most vibrant."

"And arrogant. My father had more sensitivity in his baby finger than Greg Senior had in his entire body." Casting him a venomous look, she paused only for Frederick to unlock the door before storming into the house. "My mother knew that. No, she didn't use your father. It was the other way around. He was going through a midlife crisis and needed to know that women still found him attractive." Rounding the newel post, she began the climb from the basement to the first floor of the general living quarters. "What better way than to seduce his best friend's wife?"

"Seduce? Hah!" Greg was close on her heels. "And if she was so appreciative of her husband, why was she available? Hmm? How about an answer there?"

"He was a very attractive man, and she was human. Maybe she wasn't as strong as she might have been, but nothing would have happened if he'd left her alone." With the stairs behind her, Diandra strode angrily toward the living room. "She was old-fashioned. She wouldn't have dared initiate anything like that on her own."

"Dream on, little girl."

She whirled on him with her hands on her hips. "It's the truth."

"Says who?" Greg shot back. His hands, too, were on his hips, and his eyes were dark with fury. "You were fifteen at the time. You mean to tell me that your mother told you everything she was doing and feeling?"

"I was sixteen for at least part of that affair, and I know what I do because my father spent hours talking with me after she died."

"Do you honestly think he'd tell you that your mother was a willing cheat? He couldn't admit that he'd failed her himself. So he blamed my dad."

"He *knew* your dad!" Diandra shouted. Turning on her heel, she went to the fireplace. "They were best friends for years and years. My mother a cheat?" She raised a hand to the mantel for support. "Oh, no, you've got it backward. Your dad was the cheat, and it wasn't only with my mother—" She broke off.

"Hold it. Hold it right there. You'd better think twice before you repeat that—"

His warning ended abruptly and was replaced by a thick silence. He went as still as Diandra, his gaze having joined hers, fixed on the ornate marble mantel, on a velvet box that sat there. It was slim, about six inches square and open. Nestled in its gentle velvet folds was a necklace so exquisite that it was a minute before either of them was able to speak.

3

W hat is it?'' Diandra finally whispered.

Greg didn't know what to say. It was obviously a
necklace, but that was where the obvious ended. He
had never seen anything like it. On the bed of velvet
lay one emerald teardrop after another, linked by diamond clusters and fine gold filigree to form a graceful circle. At the top was an intricate diamond-and-
gold clasp. At the bottom, the throat, the emeralds
paired up to descend in a plait that ended in twin
fringes of diamond.

He guessed there to be twenty emeralds, each the
size of one of Diandra's polished fingernails, and
though far smaller, nearly sixty diamonds. Gemstone
to gemstone, each was perfect, but the breathtaking
thing was what they became together. Captured light
shimmered between them. With the emeralds for
strength, the diamonds for brilliance and the gold for
delicacy, the necklace was a goddess of a gem. It fairly
pulsed from its velvet bed.

It didn't take a connoisseur of fine jewels to know
that the necklace was priceless.

Diandra reached out to touch it, but just short of
their goal, her fingers hovered, then drew back. She

curled them into a fist, pressed the fist to her chest. "Whose is it?" she whispered.

"I don't know," Greg answered on a mixed note of puzzlement and awe. "I've never seen it before."

She leaned closer to study the gold setting around one of the emeralds. "It looks old. Do you think it was Emma's?" Emma, Bart's first wife, had been dead for twenty-five years.

Greg shook his head. "If it had been Emma's, it would have been bequeathed either to my mother or my aunt, in which case I'd have seen it—and remembered seeing it—before. But I haven't."

"Not on Dotty or Pauline?" Dotty had been Bart's second wife, Pauline his third. Old Bart had outlived them both.

Again Greg shook his head. "Not even in pictures. And I would have remembered. It would take a certain kind of woman to wear a necklace like this. Neither Dotty nor Pauline could have pulled it off. They'd have been totally overshadowed." He paused. "Besides, Bart's a show-off. If any of his wives had owned a necklace like this, you can bet we'd all have known it."

Diandra ached to touch the necklace but didn't dare. "It's very beautiful. Almost . . . alive."

Greg was thinking the same thing. "What's it doing here?" he asked in the same quiet, almost reverent tone.

Shrugging, she peered around and behind the box "There's no note."

"It's just sitting. Waiting."

"Where did it come from?"

It was Greg's turn to shrug.

"Maybe Frederick knows," she mused. The thing to do would be to ask him, she knew, but she didn't move from where she stood. She couldn't take her eyes off the necklace. It intrigued her.

Greg was similarly spellbound. "Whose *is* it?" he whispered.

"I don't know," she whispered back, "but it shouldn't be lying around this way. Anyone could just walk in and take it. It must be worth an incredible amount."

"I hope Bart's insured."

"I hope he knows it's here."

"He has to know. This is his house. What's in it is his."

Diandra thought about that, then frowned. "Strange that he wouldn't have mentioned it. I mean, I'm sure the Waterford's valuable, and the Chippendale chairs and the Daumier prints, but this has to be even more so." She opened her palm on her chest, then moved her hand to the mantelpiece not far from the box. "So why's it sitting out here like this?"

"I don't know."

"It should be in a safe."

Greg moved closer to the necklace. That movement also brought him close enough to Diandra to catch gentle wisps of her perfume. He found both her scent and the closeness to be pleasant. "Bart has a safe in the den," he said. "I suppose we could put it there."

She bit her lip. "Seems a shame."

He knew. "Like burying something alive."

Just then, from beneath the living room arch, Frederick cleared his throat. "Excuse me." They whirled around, but he seemed oblivious to having intruded on anything out of the ordinary. "I've put your bag in the wicker room, Miss Diandra. Sir, yours is in the oak room."

Diandra gave him a puzzled look. Gregory frowned, got his bearings then asked, "Frederick, what's this doing here?"

Frederick stood stock still. "What's . . . what doing here?" he asked, as always enunciating his words with care.

"The necklace," Diandra said.

"What necklace?"

Diandra and Greg looked at each other before turning back toward the mantel. Only then did Frederick look beyond them.

"Oh, my," he murmured and took a step forward.

"Whose is it?" Diandra asked.

He looked totally befuddled. "I have no idea."

"You didn't put it here?"

"No, I did not."

Gregory found that hard to believe. "But you're the only one living here."

"Living here, yes. Working here, no. There's Mrs. Potts, who comes in twice a week to clean, and Dominic, who works with the plants and the window boxes. Then, of course, there's young Miss Connolly from the office, who drops by every so often at Mr. Bartholomew's request to work with the books in his desk."

"So if you didn't put the necklace here," Diandra said, "one of them might have."

"I did not put the necklace there, miss."

"Have you ever seen it before?" Greg asked.

"No, sir."

"Then it had to have been put here while you were picking us up."

"Not necessarily," Frederick said. "I had no cause to be in this room today. The last time I was here was when I came in to polish the andirons yesterday morning."

"And the necklace wasn't here then?"

"It was not."

Diandra fell quiet. Her eyes were on the necklace, drawn there and held by something even beyond the beauty of the piece. Gregory, too, studied it in silence. He had to make an effort to recall the many questions that remained.

"So," he stated quietly, "one of those others had to have put it here. Which of them were in this room between the time you were here yesterday and now?"

Frederick tipped up his chin and stood very straight. Even then, the top of his head barely reached the level of Greg's chin, but what he lacked in height, he made up for in starch. "Mrs. Potts was here. And Miss Connolly." He paused, then murmured another "Oh, my."

"What is it?" Diandra asked.

Frederick looked distinctly uncomfortable, as though at that moment his own starch chafed. The tips of his ears turned pink, and he cleared his throat. "The gentlemen were here last evening."

"What gentlemen?"

He paused before answering. "Mr. Bartholomew's friends."

His uncharacteristic hesitancy puzzled Greg. "What friends?"

"Why, Mr. James, Mr. William, Mr. Louis and Mr. John."

That told Greg nothing. Old Bart had a large coterie of friends and acquaintances, with any number of men named James, William, Louis and John among them. Frederick would be able to fill in the last names, but for the moment another question seemed more pressing. "What were they doing here without Bart?"

Diandra, too, was looking at Frederick—with the same interest Greg felt. That interest piqued when Frederick seemed loath to answer. "What's going on, Frederick?" she asked.

Frederick craned his neck. "Nothing really, miss. Those friends of Mr. Bartholomew's meet here from time to time."

"Without Bart knowing?" Greg asked.

"Oh, Mr. Bartholomew knows."

"What do they do here?"

"They sit."

"Just sit?" Greg asked.

"They talk."

Diandra tipped her head. "Why here?" The butler didn't answer. "Frederick?"

Perhaps in search of a sympathetic male, Frederick chose to look at Greg, which was a mistake. Greg's expression was commanding. Frederick spoke. "The gentlemen in question are all retired and have wives who are...shall we say, repressive. Therefore the gentlemen come here once every few weeks."

"To do what?" Greg asked, though the question had been asked and answered before. He sensed Frederick had withheld a noteworthy piece of information—and he was right.

Looking slightly pinched, Frederick admitted, "They play poker."

Diandra tipped back her head and whispered, "Ahhhh."

Greg simply looked smug. "I take it," he said, "that they aren't playing for pennics?"

"Not quite," Frederick answered archly.

With that particular mystery solved, Greg and Diandra exchanged a glance. "One of them may have left the necklace," she suggested.

"As a stake?"

They looked at Frederick. He shook his head. "These gentlemen deal in stocks. Not jewelry. And I am sure that one of them would have reported having seen this necklace if it had been here then. Despite their...habit...they are honorable men."

Having always thought of Frederick as a man of high standards, Diandra was prepared to take his word for that. "But if they were here last night and made no mention to you of the necklace," she reasoned, "someone had to have put it here this morning. Were both Mrs. Potts and Miss Connolly here today?"

"Only Mrs. Potts," Frederick said, then raised his nose a fraction. "Of course, I have no way of knowing whether one of those others entered while I was either at the market this morning or at the airport this afternoon. They all possess keys."

The obvious course to take would be to call each of them. The even more obvious course to take would be to call Bart. Diandra knew it, just as Greg did, yet neither suggested either course. Instead, they let their eyes be drawn back to the necklace.

After several long moments of silence, Frederick asked, "Will there be anything else?"

Greg shook his head.

"Dinner will be served at seven. Perhaps you'd like to make yourselves comfortable until then?" Without awaiting an answer, he executed an efficient turn and left the room.

Both pairs of eyes remained on the necklace.

"It really is beautiful," Diandra whispered. Again she wanted to touch it, but something held her back. "Strange," she said, then caught her breath when the necklace seemed to sparkle in response.

Greg raised a hand. His long fingers came to rest on the edge of the case. He extended them, drew them back just shy of contact, let them lie lightly on the velvet.

"Greg?"

"It's okay."

"You were going to touch it, but you changed your mind."

"No." He hadn't actually changed his mind. He'd been about to touch it and...something...had stopped him. "It just seems so incredibly valuable."

"You've touched valuable things before."

"This is different. There's an aura to this thing."

Aura was a good word for it, she decided. The necklace was mesmerizing. "Do you think," she whispered, trying to pass the eeriness of the situation off with humor, "that if you touch it a puff of smoke will rise up and spew out a genie?"

"Don't be dumb," he murmured back.

"Maybe you'll turn to stone."

"Not quite."

"Then touch it. I dare you."

They were standing so close that the slightest whisper could be heard by the other. Suddenly, though, Greg took a full breath, drew himself straighter and said in a normal voice, "This is ridiculous! It's just a necklace!"

Diandra jumped at the sound, then felt foolish. To compensate, she scowled up at him, which was a mistake. She was stunned to find him so close, so tall, large and imposing. Resentful of the fact that he made her feel small, she snapped, "What did you *think* it was?"

He scowled back. "I didn't know *what* to think, what with the way you were whispering, like it was some kind of sacred thing."

"It's just a necklace," she said, echoing his words, but she wondered who she was trying to convince. "Touch it. It won't bite."

"Why haven't *you* touched it?"

"Because I know the need you have." Her voice hardened. "You've always had it, Greg. Remember when we were kids and Bart's brother, your great-uncle Sam, bought a new horse for the farm in upstate New York? There were probably eight of us standing around, *dying* for a ride, but we stood back and waited because we knew that if you weren't the first one up, there'd be hell to pay. You always had to be the first to touch things. It never mattered that you walked away soon after, but you needed to put your mark there."

Greg felt his hackles rise. "Are you kidding? I was the only one with the *guts* to get on that horse."

"Guts, my foot. It was sheer machismo. You were a chauvinist from the time you were twelve!"

"And you were a pain in the butt!" he snapped. With a last scathing look at her, he lowered his gaze to the necklace. Instantly he felt calmer.

Diandra saw that change. Frowning, she, too, looked at the necklace, and the same calm she'd seen, she felt.

Without further ado, Greg touched it. He put a fingertip to one emerald, traced its teardrop shape, let two other fingertips join the first and move over the diamond-and-gold lacework.

"How does it feel?" Diandra whispered.

"Warm," he whispered back. "Why is it warm?"

She had no answer. April in Boston was that awkward time when it was too mild outside to turn up the heat but still too cool for air conditioning. The living room that early evening was on the chilly side. The gems should have transmitted that.

With great care, Greg slid his fingers under the stones and lifted the necklace from its box. It was surprisingly pliant, a credit to the skill of the goldsmith who had crafted the filigree links. The emeralds spread over his palm, their green seeming richer than rich, and the diamonds kept up a steady stream of sparkle.

Unable to resist, Diandra touched an emerald—very lightly and only for a minute, but one touch wasn't enough. Her hand came back, fingertips creeping over that emerald, and another, and a cluster of diamonds, as though they were braille and held a message for her. Their warmth was augmented by that of Greg's skin.

"What should we do with it?" she asked softly.

"We could leave it here until we make some calls."

"That seems risky."

"We could put it in the safe."

But she felt the same hesitancy she'd felt earlier, and when she gave the tiniest of headshakes, Greg agreed.

"You could wear it," he suggested.

"Oh, no. I couldn't do that."

"Sure you could."

"But it's not mine."

"You could wear it for safety's sake."

For safety's sake, she knew, they should lock it up in the den. It seemed so precious, not quite fragile, since the emeralds exuded too much strength for that, but certainly old and of great worth. The safe would be the way to go. But why did she get an odd feeling of suffocation when she thought of that?

Greg took one deep breath, then another. "We'll leave it here for now—at least until we call Bart."

Diandra was comfortable with that decision. "The outside doors are all locked, and Bart's alarm system is very effective." She gave the smallest, inadvertent emphasis to the "very," but it was enough to arouse Greg's curiosity.

He looked down past the smooth raven cap of her hair to her face. "You've had experience with it?"

She shot him a single sheepish glance. "Oh, yes."

He waited. When she didn't elaborate, he said, "I must have missed that story."

In another time and place, Diandra would have done her best to neatly change the subject. But just then she was feeling amiable. "Nothing to miss. Caroline, Susan and I were here with our folks. We were fourteen and feeling our oats. We wanted to see what Boston was like at night—like at one or two—so we snuck out."

"And the alarm went off."

"Not when we left. Our parents were all asleep, but apparently Bart was still out—he was between wives at the time—so the alarm hadn't been activated for the night."

Greg knew what was coming. "While you were out, he came back, thought everyone was in, turned on the alarm and went to bed." His voice was that of experience. "You should have climbed the chestnut tree in the courtyard and crawled in the pantry window. None of the windows were wired back then. It was a pretty primitive system."

Diandra should have figured that he'd have been in a similar mess and found a way out—or in, in this case. Somehow, though, she wasn't annoyed. Her thoughts were on that long-ago night. "Primitive it may have been, but was it ever loud! There were the three of us, groping madly in the dark for the switch to turn the thing off, when Bart came down the stairs and switched on the light. Everyone in the house was awake. Half the *neighborhood* was awake. Our parents were furious." She paused for a breath, then added in a small voice, "And you never heard about it?"

Greg allowed a crooked smile. "Nope. I never heard."

As odd as Diandra thought that, because she'd imagined Greg to have a running list of every faux pas she'd made in life, she found his smile to be even more odd. It was gentle. She couldn't remember ever having received a gentle smile from him before, and she'd have remembered. It touched her somewhere deep inside.

The smile faded. Greg wasn't sure where it had come from—certainly not from the alarm incident, because it wasn't *that* funny. But what puzzled him was the look on Diandra's face. If he hadn't known better, he'd have said she needed that smile. But that was perfectly absurd, he knew. Diandra didn't need anything. She was independent and self-sufficient, and when she wanted a man, she had her pick of the Washington crop. She didn't need his smile. She didn't need *him*. Which just went to show how wrongly certain looks could be interpreted.

Dropping his gaze to the necklace, which was a glowing thing winding across his palm and through his fingers, he felt instantly soothed. "Want a drink?" he asked quietly.

"I . . . uh-huh."

He reached for the velvet box, but rather than putting the necklace inside, he carried both with him from the living room and down the hall toward the back of the house, where Bart's den was tucked neatly behind the stairs.

Stopping at the desk, he set down the box and very carefully returned the necklace to it. Then he stood there for a minute, holding the hand that had held the necklace so it wouldn't feel so empty.

Diandra felt that emptiness. Confused by it, she pressed her own hands together and went to the bar. She was about to reach for the bottle of Scotch when Greg asked, "Any wine?"

Surprised, she looked up. Greg wasn't a heavy drinker. She couldn't remember ever having seen him high, much less drunk. But when he did drink, he drank Scotch. "Uh . . ." She ran an eye over the assortment of bottles, grabbed a tall one by its slender neck and separated it from the rest. "I don't know how long it's been here."

"It'll be fine." Shrugging out of his jacket, he let it drop over a corner of the sofa. He loosened his tie as he sat down, then, sinking even lower, stretched out his legs and crossed his ankles.

Unable to help herself, Diandra studied him. His hair wasn't all that bad. It was really quite attractive. *He* was really quite attractive...dashing looking... though he seemed half-asleep.

"You look the way I feel," she said. There was no sarcasm in her voice or in her manner as she handed him a glass of wine. Nor, as she stood over him, did she feel—or wish to feel—any superiority. At that moment, she identified with him. They were on the same side of an undesirable situation.

Taking the glass from her fingers, he lowered it to his lap, changed his mind, raised it and took a drink, then met her gaze. "It's been a lousy couple of days." And it seemed to be catching up with him. Relaxed was one word for what he felt, lethargic a second, drained a third. He concentrated on relaxed.

With her own glass of wine in hand, Diandra settled into the large side chair. It, too, was of aged leather, and though it didn't have quite the cushiony plushness that the sofa did, it had the wing back she loved. She'd always felt secure in it.

"Did you get everything taken care of?" she asked.

"No. There'll probably be a couple of frantic calls coming in while I'm here." He leaned his head against the sofa back to study her. "How about you?"

"The same. I spent most of Sunday in the office, for whatever good that did. Things were pretty hectic when I ran out of there this afternoon. This afternoon?" She rolled her eyes. "It seems longer than that since I left."

Greg was thinking the same thing. He glanced at the ship's clock on the wall and discovered that barely three hours had passed since he'd left New York. When he reviewed, act by act, what had taken place during each of those hours, the timing was right. Still, somehow, it seemed longer—almost as though someone had called "Cut!" in the middle and taken a lengthy break before resuming action.

Seeking out the necklace, which was propped regally on the desk, he took a deep breath, then a slow sip of wine. The pale liquid lingered on his tongue. Then he looked at Diandra and asked in a perplexed tone, "How did we get ourselves into this?"

She nestled into a corner of the wing back and said quietly, "Bart set us up. I think he plotted it, right down to my late plane last Saturday. That rattled me, and *that* suited his purpose." She paused, thought. "He's a crafty old guy. The craftiest thing he did was getting us down to Palm Beach together. It wouldn't have worked if he hadn't done that. Confronted separately, we'd have come up with excuses."

"We did come up with excuses."

"But we didn't use them with any kind of force."

"I don't know," he mused in a moment's dry humor. "I thought you were using a little force there for a while."

She gave a soft snort. "I almost did myself in."

He grinned, which in turn made her bristle.

"I don't see anything funny in that," she told him. "I wasn't doing anything more than you wanted to do but were afraid to—"

"I was not afraid," he corrected, all humor vanishing.

"Sure looked it to me."

"I was being prudent."

"Well, the end result was the same. You left me standing there alone. I nearly took the fall for saying what you were feeling."

"Haven't we been through this before?"

"Apparently it's not settled."

"Fine," Greg said. "Let's settle it, then. What happened to you in Palm Beach was your own mouth, your own doing. You've always been too impulsive for your own good."

"That's called spontaneity, and it's gotten me where I am. Your dark, silent approach is limiting."

"It's worked for me."

"It may be fine for New York, where cold sophistication scores, but believe me, it's not right for San Francisco."

"And that's what this is all about, isn't it?" He came forward in his seat, eyes dark gray and direct. "There wouldn't be any problem if you'd just settle down in Washington. What in the devil do you want with a new store?"

He might as well have said, "Why don't you be a good girl and stay in the kitchen where you belong," for the effect his words had on Diandra. Furious, she set her wineglass down hard on the desk. In the process, though, the necklace caught her eye and she paused. Greg followed her line of sight. He, too, grew quiet. Their anger seemed to float upward and dissipate, as though it had been in a balloon that had popped.

Diandra felt a gradual easing in her body. Slipping her feet from her shoes, she curled her legs beneath her skirt. She took up her wineglass again and returned her head to the lush burgundy leather. Her gaze made a leisurely sweep of the room, making stops from time to time, pensive.

"I wish he weren't selling," she said in a soft voice. "I always liked this place." After a minute, she added an even quieter "Especially this room."

Greg agreed. He didn't have to look around to see the shelves filled to overflowing with books, the assorted memorabilia that covered every other free space, the blotter on the desk, the silver inkwell. In his mind, the den had always been a retreat. It was masculine but warm, as exemplified by the twin tall lamps covered with burgundy shades that stood on either side of the massive desk and cast a soft light about the room.

"What's your place like in Washington?" Greg heard himself ask. He wasn't sure where the question had come from, but it didn't seem out of place. Apparently Diandra didn't feel it was either, because she answered with little more than a wry smile.

"Not as nice as this." She raised a hand. "No, maybe that's wrong. It's just different from this. This town house is old and stately. It holds a world of memories. My place is in a building that was totally rehabbed four years ago. I'd been living in an apartment for the year before that, and I thought the condo would be heaven." She shot a glance at the ceiling in self-mockery. "Well, it isn't. It's modern and elegant, but somewhere in the rehab process it lost its character. When I had one of our decorators do it up for me, it lost even *more* character."

She frowned at her wine, trying to think of the words to explain to Greg what she felt about both that condo and Washington. Finally she raised her head. "My place is very pretty, but it has none of the personal feeling this place has, and I miss that."

Greg was silent for a long while, thinking that she'd voiced the major complaint he had about his own place. It was weird that she'd done that, weird that she felt the same thing. Then again, maybe her problem was simple unfamiliarity. Between the hours she put in at work and the time she no doubt spent elsewhere, her condominium was probably little more than a dress stop.

What puzzled him most, though, was not that she lacked an attachment to her place, but that it bothered her. He'd have thought that as long as the social whirl went on, she wouldn't mind.

"And you?" she asked. When he eyed her distractedly, she added, "Your place in New York."

"Oh. It's okay. High-rise condo. Chic. Every amenity."

"So enthusiastic," she mocked.

"It's fine. Really."

When he said nothing more, she yielded to the silence. It was surprisingly comfortable, surprisingly free of the competitive edge that usually abraded the air between them. Her gaze wandered to the desktop, to the dark velvet box with its brilliant inhabitant, and she felt an odd kind of peace.

Greg, too, felt that peace, which was why only curiosity was in his voice when he asked, "Do you really want San Francisco?"

She rubbed the wineglass against her bottom lip and said over its rim, "Yes, I want it."

"Why?"

She lowered the glass and shrugged. "The change. The challenge. It must be the same with you."

The tiny movement of his head said it was. "Do you know many people out there?" He wondered if there were boyfriends waiting.

She shook her head. "I've met a few people over the years through business, but they're strictly acquaintances. I do have two friends, girls who were on my Europe trip when I graduated from high school. They were good to me," she said. What she didn't say was that Maren and Lyn had been understanding of the pain she was feeling that summer over her mother's death. "It's been a long time, but we've kept in touch. They're both living in the Bay area, both married, both mothers." She ran out of things to say, and her words seemed to hang in the air for a moment too long.

Greg wondered if she ever missed being a wife and mother. He was thinking of one or two pithy comments he could make about that when his eyes fell on the necklace. Those comments seemed suddenly wrong.

"It has a history," Diandra whispered. "I can feel it. The vibes are phenomenal."

Greg agreed. Every time he looked at the thing, he felt something odd. The necklace made him stop, reconsider, grow mellow. Needing suddenly to understand what power it held, he came to his feet, turned the phone around on the desk and dialed Palm Beach.

Gretchen greeted him warmly, but when he asked to speak with Bart, she was unable to help. "Why, he's left."

Greg shot a glance at Diandra. "Left?" She was up in a minute, pressing her ear to the phone beside his.

"Set out this morning, they did, Mr. Nicholas Stuttingham and he," Gretchen went on. "At this minute, they are on Mr. Nicholas's boat heading for the Caribbean. As Mr. Bart told it to me, they will be out of touch for the next two weeks."

"Out of touch?" Greg echoed. "Bart's an old man, for goodness' sake. What if he needs a doctor?"

"I asked the same question, I did, and he did not appreciate my askin' it. He said that there was a full crew aboard Mr. Nicholas's boat, and that if there were to be any emergency, they would have adequate means of getting help."

Diandra drew back her head, only to exchange a glance with Greg and whisper, "He can send messages but not receive them. Doesn't that strike you as being convenient?"

"Very," he whispered back, then said into the phone, "Gretchen, do you know anything about a necklace?"

"A necklace?"

"A very old and beautiful one of emeralds and diamonds that has mysteriously shown up here at the town house."

"I don't know about any necklace."

Greg prodded her a bit, but it was clear she was speaking the truth. When he hung up the phone, he studied Diandra in silence. They were standing very close again, but it seemed appropriate. Bart had something up his sleeve, and they were allies.

"*Crafty* is one word for him," Greg mused, employing the word Diandra had used earlier.

"How can he be out of touch? Even aside from the necklace, doesn't he know that we'll have dozens of questions to ask him during the week?"

"He must have done it on purpose. He wants this place closed up, but he doesn't want any part of the closing."

Casting a look around the room, Diandra didn't blame him. Just thinking about dismantling this home made her lonely. She was glad Greg was standing close. The warmth of his body was something that would remain when all the rest had been crated and sealed.

Without moving away, she met his gaze and asked quietly, "What next? Do we call Mrs. Potts?"

At that moment, confronting her upturned face, Greg didn't want to make another call. An image had entered his mind and was crowding out most else. "We'll let Frederick do that," he said distractedly. "He knows how to be discreet."

"And the necklace?"

They looked at the object in question. As he'd done before, Greg carefully lifted it from its bed. After a long minute, he looked at Diandra. "Put it on."

She raised a hand to her throat. It was bare, save a single strand of pearls that fell loosely around the open collar of her silk blouse. She was about to repeat that she'd be uncomfortable wearing the necklace when she realized that wasn't so. Something in a corner of her mind was telling her that the jewels belonged around her neck.

Silently she removed the strand of pearls. But when Greg began to work at the necklace's clasp, an irregularity on the back caught her eye. She touched his hand, said, "Wait," and turned over the clasp to reveal a crest and an inscription delicately etched in the gold. "A. avec amour, C."

She'd been reading in a hushed voice. When she reached the end, she raised her eyes to Greg's and breathed, "Incredible."

"I know," he whispered. It looked as though the necklace hadn't belonged to a York at all; the initials were wrong.

"It has a real history. Look at that crest."

Greg looked. "Makes you wonder about the story behind it...."

"Who made it—"

"Who owned it—"

"Where it's been—"

"What it's lived through. Two hundred years worth of events—"

"And romance. Incredible."

The look in her eyes was so soft that Greg had to tear his gaze away. As quickly as he could, he finished releasing the clasp and moved behind Diandra to secure the necklace. Then he turned her around so that he could see.

Fortunately she remained quiet, because if she'd asked for a rational answer to a rational question at that moment, he'd have been unable to give it. The necklace, resting on her warm, ivory-hued skin, was exquisite. But what held him speechless was Diandra herself. *She* was exquisite. She was soft and beautiful, gentle and giving, but strong. She was, at that moment, everything a woman should be. And more. She was, at that moment, simultaneously the most innocent and sexy woman he'd ever seen. And at that moment, he wanted her.

4

Diandra felt shaky as she lay in bed that night. As though it had happened two minutes before, rather than several hours, she recalled the instant Greg had fastened the necklace around her neck, turned her around and looked at her. In that instant, like a bolt out of the blue, she'd felt an intense wave of desire.

It had passed. She'd made sure of that by withdrawing into herself and continually, if silently, repeating every reason why she *couldn't* want Gregory York—the most notable one being that she didn't *like* Gregory York.

Fortunately Greg hadn't been talkative himself. They'd eaten dinner largely in silence, and soon after, she'd excused herself and gone upstairs. She'd showered and put on the old football jersey that she used as a nightshirt, expecting to be out like a light when her head hit the pillow.

Tired as she was, though, she couldn't sleep. It didn't matter that she kept her mind diverted—her body had a will of its own. It seemed to be reverberating from that bolt out of the blue.

For two hours—she knew, because she looked at the bedside clock every ten minutes—she tossed and turned. Finally she climbed from bed and went to the window. But the night was dark, and there was little by way of entertainment on Chestnut Street late at night.

Chancing to glance back over her shoulder, she caught sight of the emerald necklace. It lay in a slender beam of moonlight, glittering more gently than before. Almost on whim, she took it from where it lay on the nightstand and fastened it around her neck. Then she sat in the wicker rocker, covered herself with the afghan that had been lying at the foot of the bed and rocked herself to sleep.

When she awoke in the morning, she felt vaguely stiff. She had moved from the rocker to the bed at four, but the damage had been done. On top of that, she was disoriented. The quaint wicker room in Bart's town house was a far cry from her bedroom in D.C. The decor was different, the light, the sounds. It took her a minute to remember where she was and why. On the tail of that awareness, she let out a groan.

She didn't want to be in Boston. She didn't want to be closing up the town house. She didn't want to be doing it with Greg.

Then she put her hand to her neck.

The necklace was there, warm to the touch. It didn't help her stiffness, but just touching it put her in a better frame of mind to face the day.

After taking a long, hot shower that soothed her aches some, she put on a shirt and jeans and went downstairs. Greg was in the kitchen, perched on a stool at the center island. He was dressed much as she was in an old shirt and jeans, but his seemed to positively stroke his large frame. His shirt was open at the collar and rolled at the sleeves, and the tails hung low over jeans that had worn soft and faded. He looked far more attractive than any man had a right to look so early in the morning and far more attractive than Gregory York had a right to look *any* time.

She could handle it, she told herself. She could handle the way he looked, because he'd always been gorgeous. And she knew that what she'd felt the night before hadn't been real. What she couldn't quite handle was the way he was looking her over. He wasn't leering; if he'd done that, she might have produced a little anger to use as a shield. But he was eyeing her with curiosity that verged on wariness.

"Something wrong?" she asked, doing her best to hold still beneath his scrutiny.

Slowly he shook his head, but his eyes continued their journey over her body. He was proving a point to himself—that what he'd felt the night before hadn't been desire but simple appreciation. Yes, he appreciated Diandra's looks. Who wouldn't? She could add elegance to a potato sack simply by the way she stood. Of course, she wasn't wearing a potato sack. She was wearing jeans that fitted her snugly and a shirt that was stylishly loose. And her face was totally devoid of makeup, which made him appreciate her natural beauty all the more.

So he appreciated her. Did he desire her?

"What are you *staring* at?" she asked with a sudden scowl.

"You." No, he didn't desire her. He couldn't desire a woman who was so quick to vex. Besides, he didn't *like* her, and in the eighties, a man didn't desire a woman he didn't like.

She glanced down at herself. "Do I have toothpaste on my shirt or torn jeans or mismatched sneakers?" When her eyes rose, his were focused on her breasts. She felt her skin prickle, and she was beginning to fear she was in trouble when he lifted his eyes to the necklace.

Instantly his expression softened. "Still have it on?"

Expelling a tiny sigh of relief, she put a hand to her throat. "I thought we agreed I should wear it. For safety's sake."

For the safety of the necklace, that was right, Greg knew. With Diandra wearing it, they always knew where it was. For his own safety, ah, that was something else. The necklace definitely did something—to her, to him, he wasn't sure. When he looked at that necklace he found it harder to remember that he disliked her.

Hard, but not impossible. Nothing was impossible, he told himself. "You didn't wear it in the shower, did you?"

"Of course not."

"Did you sleep with it on?"

She nodded. "It's a powerful narcotic."

"You needed one?"

Diandra didn't like his tone of voice. "No. I'd have fallen asleep without it, but I was in a strange bed and it helped." Anxious to change the subject—lest he probe more deeply into the cause of her unrest—she tucked her hands into the rear pockets of her jeans and eyed the cup of coffee he was nursing. "Who made it?" she asked cautiously.

He followed her gaze. "Me."

Instantly she headed for the cabinet. "Thank goodness. Frederick happens to make the worst coffee I've ever tasted."

"You haven't ever tasted mine," Gregory warned. Actually the coffee he'd made was probably fine full strength, but in deference to his stomach, he'd laced his own cup heavily with milk. He didn't particularly care for the taste of it that way, but he needed coffee in the morning, so weak it was.

Diandra wasn't being fussy, either. Figuring that she was going to have to be on her toes to survive a full day with Greg, she reached for a mug and filled it with the steaming dark brew. She was appalled to find that her hands shook, appalled to realize that Greg rattled her so. She was even more appalled to think that it wasn't just one day with him that she had to survive.

Cradling the mug between both palms, she leaned back against the counter and set herself to thinking "confident and composed."

Greg waited. He watched her raise the mug to her lips, take a sip, then lower it. "Well?" he asked.

For a minute she drew a total blank. She couldn't remember his having asked a question. She tried to replay the conversation, but it was only when he dropped a pointed gaze to her mug that she realized what he wanted to know. "Oh. It's fine. Very good."

"Where were you just then?"

She wasn't about to tell him that she'd been in her private locker room giving herself a pep talk, so she shrugged and said, "It's taking me a few minutes to wake up," which wasn't a total lie.

"Are you always slow first thing in the morning?" he asked, wondering if he should note that for future reference. He never knew when a moment of slowness would come in handy where Diandra was concerned.

"Actually," she answered, surprised as she thought about it, "I'm usually pretty quick. The minute I wake up, my mind shifts into gear." She raised the mug to her lips, took a sip, then frowned. "I feel like I'm on hold. It's odd not going into the office."

"Pretend it's a weekend."

"Weekend or not, I work."

"*All* the time?" he asked skeptically.

"No, not all the time. But when I'm not working, my mind isn't far from it. I feel a little...lost right now." As soon as she said the words, she feared she'd been too revealing. It had always struck her as important to keep up a strong front before Greg. So she added hastily, "I guess that's because I've never done anything like packing up a house before." She wrinkled her nose. "Aren't there professionals who do this kind of thing? Shouldn't we have someone in to appraise things?"

Greg wished she wouldn't wrinkle her nose. When she did that, she looked innocent and adorable—which, surely, she knew, which, surely, was why she did it. All he had to do was to remind himself that the look was for show and he was safe.

Unfortunately the look had an effect before he could do the reminding. His voice came out a little more throaty than usual when he said, "Eventually we should," in response to her question. Then he took a deep breath and straightened his shoulders; that made him feel better, more his capable, formidable self. "For now we're on our own." He tossed a glance toward the large industrial stove that was polished to a high chrome sheen. "And I mean, *really* on our own. The cook's gone. I sent him out for cartons."

Diandra nodded. There seemed no point in getting ruffled that Greg had taken command. She'd obviously slept later than he had, and they did need cartons. So he'd sent Frederick after them. It made sense. The sooner they got to work, the sooner they'd finish and the sooner she could return to Washington.

Greg was watching the play of emotions on her face. "Any problem?" he asked when she'd been quiet a little too long.

"No, no."

"You do know how to make breakfast, don't you?"

"Of course."

"So what do you want?"

"Uh...I don't usually eat much. Maybe some toast."

He gave her a look as he rose from the stool and muttered, "I need more than that." Opening the refrigerator, he rummaged through its contents.

Diandra, meanwhile, moved to the far side of the room, to the small window seat that overlooked the courtyard. In the instant when Greg had straightened from the stool, she'd felt a flare of awareness. She was sure it had to do with the fact that, for once, she wasn't wearing high heels, so he looked taller than usual. He also looked more casual. His clothes did that, and the way he wore them. The first two buttons of his shirt were undone, which left a taunting view of tawny chest hair. His exposed forearms were ropy. His hair fell rakishly over his brow.

While she couldn't quite flee the room in a paroxysm of primness, distancing herself from him wouldn't hurt.

Propping a knee on the window cushion, she sipped her coffee and looked out. The day was overcast and not terribly cheerful. A few flowers sprouted from a whiskey barrel that Bart's neighbor had set out in his backyard, no doubt to coax spring along, but spring wasn't to be hurried. The trees in the courtyard had only the bare beginnings of buds, unlike those in Washington, which were well into bloom. It was cherry blossom time there. Now *that* was cheerful.

Having let the refrigerator swing shut, Greg was watching her. In profile, her features were delicate and very sober. He couldn't help but wonder what she was thinking. "You look like your best friend just died."

She looked quickly around, let out a small laugh and shook her head. There was no smile to accompany the laugh though, and just as quickly as she'd turned her head, she faced the window again. "The courtyard is sad," she said. "It doesn't want Bart selling this place, either."

At her mention of selling, Greg felt a pang of regret. To counter that, he tossed off a nonchalant "It'll never know the difference."

"Sure, it will. It knows who takes care of it. Bart always made sure that the chestnut tree was fed and pruned. Emma used to sweep the cobblestones, even when there was help to do that. I took my turn painting the bench." She paused and looked over her shoulder at him. "Did you ever do it?"

Coming up behind her, Greg reached out to draw the curtain farther back. "Twice. Once when I was twelve, then again when I was fourteen."

His closeness comforted her, took away some of that empty feeling. "What colors?"

"Green the first time, brown the second." They were good, solid colors. He'd been proud of his work.

Diandra let a tiny smile escape then. "I did it in red."

"You were the one? That was *hideous*."

She shrugged. "Bart said to do it in whatever color I wanted. I wanted red."

"Why?" he asked, fascinated by the mischief in her expression.

"Because it was bright and cheerful. Painted red, that bench attracted attention."

"How old were you?"

"Fifteen."

Fifteen was the age when Diandra had come into her own. Greg remembered. After a slow start, she'd become a knockout really fast. Red had definitely been her color that year.

That year also marked the start of the affair between her mother and his father. He wondered if Diandra had known at the time what was happening. Interesting that she'd chosen red. Red had been Abby's color.

Turning his back on her, Greg returned to the refrigerator, took out all he needed to make a cheese omelet and toast, then went to work fixing it. He didn't look at Diandra until he'd finished, when he threw off a quick "Want some?"

She shook her head, so he piled everything he'd made onto a single plate and, though it was truly more than he wanted, he forced himself to eat every bite— and that, purely as a matter of pride. Diandra had taken a refill of coffee and left the room before he'd finished.

A short time later, he found her in the first-floor parlor, sitting barefoot and cross-legged on the camelback settee. She had a yellow legal pad on her lap and was making notes.

"What are you doing?" he asked in a clipped tone. He stood at the door with one arm high on the jamb.

"Working." Which had always been and, she feared, would always be the antidote for her ills. The particular ill she was feeling at the moment had to do with Greg, with the moment of comfort he'd brought her in the kitchen and the abruptness with which he'd snatched it away. She could imagine why he'd done it; what she couldn't imagine was why it bothered her.

But she wasn't up for soul-searching, so she was setting to work. "I figured we should start from the bottom and work our way up. This room seemed as good a jumping-off point as any."

"What are you doing with the pad?" he demanded.

"Right now, holding it," she said, tossing his imperious tone right back at him. Then she sighed and looked around. "I guess the first thing to do is list everything that's here."

"And then?"

"I don't know—call the museum, call the appraiser, call the auction house.... Maybe call around and see if anyone else in the family wants what's here."

"Bart didn't suggest that."

"He said we should dispose of things in an appropriate fashion, but since he's opted out of the process, we'll have to use our own judgment as to what constitutes an appropriate fashion." She made a face that perfectly reflected her frustration. "He mentioned shipping some of this stuff to him, but how are we supposed to know what he wants and what he doesn't?"

Pushing away from the doorjamb, Greg sauntered across the room. "We both know that the secret to success is decisiveness." He lowered himself into a chair. "We also know that decisiveness isn't worth a damn if the person making the decision doesn't have a certain amount of basic information at his fingertips." He thrust out his bearded chin. "Well, we need more information. I'd suggest that we make your list—and make it in detail—then present it to Bart."

"He'll be gone for two weeks. We can't wait that long."

"We won't have to," Greg said succinctly.

Diandra considered that succinctness and the knowing look in his eye, and she realized he was right. Bart had never been one to cut himself off from his world for more than a few hours. He had ample means of communication from the boat. He just didn't want them to know about it.

"Okay," she conceded, "so we could reach him, but that might take time, too, and a waste of time is what we're trying to avoid. So what do we do meanwhile? He wanted things packed."

"We'll pack them, but we won't move them until Bart has gone over our lists."

"What about his buyer?"

"His buyer will wait. After all, if Bart is incommunicado for the next two weeks, his buyer won't be able to contact him, will he?" Eyeing her askance, he asked more cautiously, "You didn't catch the name of Bart's broker, did you?"

"He didn't mention it," she said. Then her eyes widened. "Do you think he was making it up?" Answering herself, she quickly shook her head. "He wouldn't have made that up, Greg. Bart isn't a liar."

"But he's crafty—to use your word. I have no doubt that he does have a buyer for this place. Whether the buyer needs to take title in two weeks, though, is the issue."

Diandra's frustration level took a jump. "But what purpose would Bart have for rushing us into this, when he knows we'd have been able to do it more comfortably at a later date?"

"He knows that given extra time we'd have come up with some scheme to get out of the job. Right?"

She let out a breath. "Right."

"But we are here, and all the speculating in the world about Bart's motives won't get the job done. Right?"

"Right."

"So." He glanced around the room. "You want to write?"

"Sure."

Starting at the archway and moving clockwise, Greg began to call off the various pieces of furniture in the parlor. There wasn't much on a large scale, since the parlor was half the size of the living room, though what there was was old and ornate. When he reached the china cabinets that were built into the wall, things grew more complex. Inside those cabinets and the drawers beneath, he found three china tea sets, numerous unmatched plates and platters, stacks of hand-stitched table linen, candles of assorted lengths and colors, and a sterling silver tea service. And that was before he began on the slew of small, original oil paintings that covered the walls.

"A woman could get writer's cramp with a job like this," Diandra remarked. She stretched her fingers.

"Too much for you?" Greg challenged.

She held up that same hand, writer's cramp ignored. "No, no. I can take it."

But Greg was wondering if *he* could. He glanced at his watch. It was only eleven. He felt as though he and Diandra had been working for hours—and they'd barely begun. There were still two other rooms on the first floor, and three full floors above them. And all they had to show for their morning was a three-page list. If he ever had a morning like that in New York, he'd hand in his resignation.

It wasn't that he was bored, just frustrated. Making lists wasn't efficient. It was what middle-level bureaucrats did to justify their positions. Making lists was a time filler, and in this case it was a poor excuse for Bart's not being there to point to this or that and say what he wanted done with it.

But more, there was the job itself. Greg didn't want to be dismantling Bart's town house. His heart wasn't in it.

He wondered what was happening at the office and why no one had called. Surely there'd been something they'd needed to ask him.

"It's so quiet here," Diandra murmured with an uncanny sense of timing. "I feel as though phones should be ringing or assistants barging in."

She had her feet on the sofa, her knees drawn up and the pad of paper propped against her thighs. It occurred to Greg that she looked perfectly comfortable that way, not at all like the executive she was. He wanted to think that she was being deliberately coy—except that she truly seemed indifferent to the pose.

"Do you kick off your shoes and tuck your legs up at work?" he asked. He tried to sound disdainful, but didn't quite make it, because more than anything just then, she looked refreshing.

"Not during the day. I don't dare then. I have an image to uphold." She gave him a sad smile. "That's the story of our lives, isn't it? Images to uphold." She looked around. "Take this room. It's a symbol, that's all. It's beautiful, the stunning facsimile of a Victorian drawing room, just as Emma intended, then Dotty, then Pauline. More than any other room in the house, this one was the epitome of social success. But we never used it much, did we?"

"It's too fussy."

"Fussy, formal, outdated... We used any other room but this."

She was right, Greg knew. When the families gathered in the town house—likewise, with the business gatherings Bart had had there over the years—the crowd generally flowed from the living room to the den, then up the stairs to the dining room and the more casual family room. He and Diandra hadn't been the only ones to find the parlor too fussy for comfort. So why had Bart kept it as it was?

"Every Boston Brahman had to have a drawing room," he said in response to his own thoughts. "It was a sign of social and financial arrival. Henry York built that first store from nothing, and Bart lived through a part of that early struggle. He needed this." A new thought popped into Greg's mind, and it was on his tongue before he could hold it back. "If the house were yours, what would you do here?"

"In this room?" Diandra asked. "Mmm, I'm not sure." She thought for a minute as she looked around, thought about what she—not a decorator—would do. Then she said with a smile, "I'd get rid of those heavy velvet drapes, strip the walls of purple flowers and auction off the furniture. Then," she took a breath, as though she were suddenly free, "I'd do up the room completely in white. White walls, white woodwork, white area rug, white furniture—soft, cushiony white furniture."

"With hands-off signs all over." Greg could picture it. There had been a room like it in his parents' house when he'd been growing up. He'd caught hell from his mother any number of times when dirt from his pockets or his socks or the cuffs of his jeans had speckled the rug.

But Diandra was shaking her head. "Everything would be washable. It would be such a soft, inviting room that people would be naturally drawn to it."

"White is virginal and forbidding."

"It's pure and warm."

"Warm? White, as in snow?"

"White, as in sun-kissed, wind-swept sand."

"That's gritty."

She shook her head. "It's smooth and soothing. Misty. No rough edges. Everything calm and peaceful."

"Ahh," he mocked. "White, as in doves. Poetic."

In the echo of his sarcasm, Diandra was reminded of just why she disliked him. He made fun of her. Granted he'd gotten more subtle with age, but he still enjoyed putting her down. "Yes, white as in doves, and it is poetic *and* beautiful. I like peace. I want little patches of it in my life. It's not my problem if you don't have the appreciation for that. And by the way, don't ask my opinion if you're going to turn around and tear it to shreds." She rose from the settee and headed for the hall.

"You won't get peace in San Francisco," he called, scrambling from his seat.

"I can try," she replied without looking back.

"Where are you going?"

"To make lunch." She was running lightly up the stairs.

He followed, though not as lightly. "At this hour?"

"I'm hungry."

"You wouldn't be hungry if you'd had breakfast."

"I wasn't hungry then."

"You should have eaten, anyway. Breakfast is the most important meal of the day."

"I'll remember that when I get to be your age," she said as she went through the kitchen door. Slapping the legal pad onto the nearest counter, she pulled open the refrigerator, from which she proceeded to take a head of lettuce, a ripe tomato, half a cucumber, a bag of shredded cheese and a plate of cold turkey.

Leaning against the doorjamb with his hands anchored in the pockets of his jeans, Greg watched her. "You're making a salad. I'm impressed."

"Why? I told you I could cook."

"Hold on. Making a salad isn't exactly cooking."

"Then why are you impressed?"

"Because it's something, and you're doing it yourself."

Not only was she doing it herself, but she was doing it deftly. With a single whack of the lettuce on the counter, she'd twisted out its core and put the head under the faucet. As soon as she set it down to drain, she took up a knife and began to do something very fast and skillful to first the cucumber, then the tomato.

For several minutes, Greg was mesmerized by the movement of her hands. Then he raised his eyes to her face, saw that her jaw was tight and guessed that nervous tension was behind much of the energy she was expending. He felt a tiny glimmer of satisfaction; it was reassuring to know that he still had the power to annoy her.

Then an emerald caught his eye. It disappeared, reappeared, disappeared, reappeared with the motion of her shirt as she worked, and it mesmerized him much as the movement of her hands had done. As he watched for it, the perverse satisfaction he'd felt was forgotten. In its place was something more gentle. Returning his eyes to Diandra's face, he felt as though he was seeing a new side, a softer side, a domestic side. It didn't replace the corporate image, but augmented it, gave it depth, made it richer.

To his chagrin, he felt his body tighten in desire.

Needing an immediate breather, he left the kitchen, trotted down two sets of stairs and went out into the courtyard. It was a damp April day, the kind that would be uncomfortably muggy if it were warmer. He was glad it wasn't warmer. He needed the slight chill to clear his head.

For a time, he ambled around the cobblestone drive. Then he propped himself against the old chestnut tree, crossed his arms over his chest and, for the first time in months, craved a cigarette.

But the craving would pass, he knew, as would that odd feeling in the pit of his stomach. He didn't desire Diandra. He couldn't. He didn't like her.

Having once more reminded himself of that fact, he took a final deep breath and went back inside. He didn't have to climb farther than the first floor; Diandra was in the living room. Again she was sitting Indian-style, this time on the chintz sofa, and she was holding one of the Oriental bowls that normally stood on a table nearby. She looked up when he appeared, carefully set the bowl aside and picked up her pad and pen.

Without a word, they went back to work. As he'd done in the parlor, Greg moved slowly around the room dictating to Diandra. He was fonder of the living room than the parlor. It had an eclectic air, created by the myriad of unusual pieces that Bart and his wives had collected over the years. He paused often to study one thing or another—a small African sculpture, an etched glass bottle, the set of French tapestry fragments that hung on the wall.

Diandra, too, found them interesting. They were also a diversion, because she was having a difficult time keeping her eyes off Greg. His legs fascinated her. They were long, lean but solid, and he moved them with an animal grace that was nearly erotic. Far more sensible, she knew, to admire a Baccarat vase.

She didn't know whether to be relieved or distressed when, far short of finishing the job, he dropped onto the far end of the sofa and scowled.

"What's wrong?" she asked.

He said nothing at first, simply sat in a slouch looking disgruntled. Not trusting his responses in the best of times, Diandra didn't push him to speak. She was almost surprised when he did.

"I don't want to be doing this," he muttered, running a hand through his hair in frustration. "It's a monumental waste of time. The house is practically a historical landmark. It shouldn't be sold." He turned cross eyes on Diandra. "Call Bart and tell him that."

"Call and tell him yourself."

"Are you enjoying this?"

"No."

"But we're locked in here." He pushed himself up and was across the floor in three long strides.

"Where are you going?" Diandra called, sitting straighter.

He disappeared, but his voice came back. "I'm hungry."

Tossing the pad aside, she jumped up and followed him. "After that breakfast you ate?"

He was taking the stairs two at a time. "That was early this morning."

"But it was huge."

"Well, I'm hungry again."

"You're just bored. The job has to be done, Greg. It won't go away."

"I know," he muttered from the top of the stairs. "I know." He continued on into the kitchen, only to pause in the middle of the floor with his hands on his hips and his head bowed. "Do you want a sandwich?"

"I just ate."

"I want a tongue sandwich."

Diandra tried not to grimace. "I don't think Frederick buys tongue. Where is he, by the way? Shouldn't he have been back by now?"

Greg's head was up, eyes focused on a slip of paper that was propped against the bowl of fruit on the counter. He crossed the floor, picked up the paper and read aloud, "'Sir, I have secured four dozen cartons, which should get you started. If you need more, please call the number attached.'"

"Four dozen?" Diandra cried in horror.

Greg silenced her with an upraised hand and read on. "'I spoke with Mrs. Potts. She knows nothing about a necklace. I have called no one else because I fear alerting too many people to the presence of something that valuable in this house.'"

"This house is *full* of valuable things," Diandra broke in to argue.

Greg dropped his gaze to the necklace, took in the creamy skin beneath it, the slenderness of the neck above it, the smoothness of Diandra's cheeks, her innocent eyes. "Not like that," he said a bit thickly, then cleared his throat and read on. " 'As no one has come looking for it or reported it missing, I see no harm in keeping it here until Mr. Bartholomew can be reached. In the meantime, I must be off.' "

"Off?" Diandra asked with a frisson of alarm.

Greg silenced her with an impatient look and went on in the deep, resonant voice that in no way resembled Frederick's. " 'I am on my way to Bermuda to see about lodging. I shall be retiring there when Mr. Bartholomew sells the town house.' "

Her eyes went wide. "On his way to Bermuda?"

" 'Best of luck with your endeavor. Your faithful servant—' "

"*Faithful!* He calls running out and leaving us here alone faithful?"

Greg wasn't any more pleased with the turn of events than she was. It was one more ominous stroke on top of the others, and it was the one that snapped what little patience he'd had. Tossing the note on top of the fruit, he turned on his heel and, brushing past Diandra, left the room.

"Now where are you going?" she yelled. He was headed upstairs, rather than down.

"Out." He'd had it with closed rooms. He'd had it with stupid assignments. And he'd had it with the faint, elusive scent that was Diandra's—and that was driving him mad.

She ran up after him. "But what about the living room?"

"It'll wait," he answered from his room.

She planted herself at the door. "Greg, we have to get this done."

He had his duffel bag on the bed and was fishing around inside. "It'll *wait*," he growled. He pulled out a small piece of slinky navy stuff, followed by a pair of goggles.

Diandra couldn't believe it. "I have a whole office on hold while I'm doing Bart's bidding, and you're going swimming? Where are you going swimming?"

"The Y," he mumbled and disappeared into the bathroom.

"You can't go swimming," she cried, but he had reappeared with a bath towel in his hand. "We have a job to do." He proceeded to roll his swimsuit and goggles in the towel.

"There's no rush." With the towel tucked under his arm, he strode past her. "We have all week."

"Come on, Greg," she protested, heading downstairs fast on his heels. "This is unfair. I'm stuck here, too, and I want to do the work and be done. You're supposed to be doing it with me. You can't just walk out and leave me alone."

At the foot of the stairs he stopped and turned so abruptly that she would have barreled into him had he not caught her arms. "Sweetheart," he growled, "if I stay here alone with you, given the way I feel right now, you'll regret it."

But Diandra wasn't thinking of regrets. She was thinking that Frederick had betrayed her by flying to Bermuda, and now, when all she wanted was to do what she'd come for and leave, Greg was betraying her, too. But then, what had she expected? "Is this how you run things in New York—by going off for a swim when the going gets tough?"

"You know damned well it isn't."

"But Boston's different," she said with narrowed, knowing eyes. "You want *me* to do the work, don't you? You want me to do it while you're gone. And here Bart thought *I* was afraid of a little hard work. Hah! Look who's afraid."

"Keep still, Diandra."

She wasn't about to do that. Eyes ablaze, she raced on. "You're thinking that if you disappear, I'll be bored enough to keep on going. Or stupid enough. Well, let me clue you in on something, mister. You can walk out of this house, and I won't be bored. There are a dozen things I can do to keep myself busy, and none of them have anything to do with Bart's job. And as for stupid—"

He tightened his hands on her arms. "That's *enough.*"

"I'm not stupid, Greg. I'm not about to do your work for you. And if you think you can scare me off with your moods, think again. Your moods don't scare me. I've been the butt of them for years."

"Not this one," he said in a quieter voice—not calmer, but quieter and more dangerous.

Diandra felt that danger. She even saw the dark gleam in his eye. But it only added to her agitation. "If it weren't for you, I wouldn't be here, but since I am, you're stuck, too. I'll be damned if I'm going to let you weasel out of your half of the work."

He tugged her closer. "You have a problem with your mouth, do you know that? It won't stay shut."

"If my mouth stayed shut, I'd be a total failure at my job. How do you think I turned that store around? By smiling sweetly at every Tom, Dick and—"

His mouth covered hers, cutting off Harry, and for a split second Diandra couldn't react. Then the second passed, and she began to push his chest, but he simply slipped an arm around her back, framed one hand to her face and held her still for his kiss.

It was as bold a kiss as she'd ever received. It molded her mouth with the force of a fine-tempered anger and refused to let the tiny sounds of protest escape from her throat. It plundered her softness, devouring the curve of her lips and the moisture within. It took her breath away and robbed her of the ability to move.

But it took Greg's breath away, too, and when he paused for air, she cried out in fury, "Gregory York! What do you think—"

He resealed her lips before she could say another word, because he didn't want to hear her anger. He'd heard enough of that to last a lifetime. What he wanted to hear were the sounds of a sweet, silky woman. That was what his mood called for, and he knew she had it in her. He also knew that she'd do her best not to respond to him that way. Which made for a very, very interesting challenge.

With that challenge foremost in his mind, his second kiss was more persuasive. His mouth stroked rather than plundered. Rather than taking as much as it could get in as short a time, it explored the same terrain in a more leisurely fashion. This second kiss was as persistent as before, but it took its force from gentleness, and that had an effect.

Diandra stopped pushing his chest. Her fury was suspended, overshadowed by unexpected sensation. She didn't willingly open her mouth to return his kiss, but the rigidity in her body eased. Without conscious intent, she leaned into him for support. And when he paused a second time for air, her voice was softer, less shrill.

"Don't do this, Greg. There's no point—"

His third kiss was even more gentle, even more powerful. Somewhere along the line he'd forgotten about punishing her for the sharpness of her tongue. He'd even forgotten about the challenge of getting her to respond. All he could think of was how good she felt in his arms, how warm and soft and woman scented, and how sweet she tasted.

Keeping one arm firmly around her back, he slid his hand along the line of her neck, moved his fingers upward into her hair, then cupped the back of her head and controlled her that way. His mouth caressed hers, exploring its fine nuances, coaxing a response for the sheer need to feel his kiss returned.

It came slowly—first in the softening of her lips, then in their opening. Despite her intentions to the contrary, Diandra couldn't help herself. She'd been kissed, but never with such deliberate care. The movement of his mouth intrigued her, as did the brush of his beard and the sleekness of his tongue. And beyond that there was his body, long and firm, pressed close, taking her weight.

It didn't matter that she didn't like him. What he was doing to her senses was addictive. One stroke demanded another, one caress a second. Though she'd always prided herself on being in control, Greg awakened a stunning hunger.

Suddenly, though, he pulled back. Taking in slow, unsteady breaths, he looked down at the flush on her lips and the moistness he'd left there. He looked at the throbbing pulse at her neck and the desire in her eyes, and he felt the satisfaction he'd sought—and then some. That was the catch. Oh, yes, he'd aroused her. But she'd also done a damned good job of arousing *him*, and that hadn't been part of the scheme.

Lowering his gaze, he focused on the necklace and not for the first time wondered what power it held. That power frightened him.

What frightened him even more, though, was the possibility that the necklace didn't have any power at all.

5

Releasing her, Greg crossed the second-floor landing and started down the next flight of stairs. The sound of his footsteps was muted by the runners that covered the oak treads, but in the silence that permeated the rest of the house, Diandra easily heard the front door open, then, seconds later, shut tight.

In the wake of his departure, she didn't move. Her heart beat loudly into the stillness, seeming to screech at her for what she'd just done. Slowly she raised a hand to her mouth and touched tentative fingertips to her lips, which were very soft, warm, moist. She dropped that hand to cover her heart in an attempt to ease its thunder, and when that didn't work, she touched the emerald necklace.

The stones were as warm as her lips had been, and though they couldn't possibly be as soft, they had that same strangely soothing effect they always had. It was as if they were telling her that everything was all right. Needing the reassurance, she remained still for another minute and let them speak.

Then, taking a single deep, if slightly unsteady breath, she went to the mahogany console that stood in the hall and stared at herself in the mirror. She was the same woman she'd always been—same hair, same skin, same eyes, nose and mouth—but something was different.

Something glowed.

It was the necklace, she reasoned. Moving her hand aside, she looked at it, but it was half-hidden by her shirt. Slowly, almost nervously, she drew her collar open and studied the way the gems lay against her skin. They looked back at her, winking smugly.

But they didn't glow.

More nervously she raised her eyes to her face. Nothing had changed; she looked the same. She tilted her head a fraction and decided that, yes, perhaps her eyes were a bit wider and her cheeks a bit more flushed. Her lips were certainly different—they still felt Greg's, still tingled.

But did they glow?

Confused, she wandered into the kitchen, but it was too full of recent memories for comfort. So she continued on into the dining room, then the family room. Without direction, she soon found herself back at the mirror.

What she saw there then wasn't a totally unfamiliar sight. But she'd never seen it reflected in the mirrored walls of CayCorp's boardroom, or in shiny store windows on the city street, or in the rearview mirror of a cab. In those places she typically saw determination on her face, perhaps concentration, satisfaction, maybe fatigue, but always confidence.

The expression she wore now was different. She'd seen it from time to time in her mirror at home, mostly at night, sometimes early in the morning. She'd seen it at those times when she was most vulnerable, when she was feeling sad and alone.

Not wanting to feel that way, she mustered a spurt of energy and ran down the stairs for her sneakers. Then she went to the closet. Her hand sped past several overcoats, a trench coat and an old, baggy golf sweater before stopping at a leather jacket that looked sufficiently large and warm. Shrugging into it, she pulled up the collar and left the house.

She walked briskly—easy to do at midafternoon when there were fewer people on the sidewalks than there would be an hour or two later. Charles Street boasted several new shops that had opened since she'd been there last, but she barely noticed. She walked on to Beacon Street, went left onto Arlington, then began a long, rapid march around her favorite spot, the public garden. She figured that if anything could occupy her mind in a positive way, that would.

It did marginally, though she half-suspected that the physical exertion more than the scenery did the trick. She kept up a rapid pace, even extending her walk up and around the common before cutting back through the webwork of paths to the garden.

Gradually she began to feel calmer and more herself. She also began to feel tired, so she found a bench that overlooked the duck pond and lowered herself to its green planks. From that vantage point she could watch the workmen spruce up the swan boats for spring.

It was there, with a cool breeze blowing against her face, that she admitted that Gregory York turned her on. It wasn't right, because she didn't like him, and there was, therefore, no future to the relationship, but he did turn her on.

And why not, she asked herself? He had all the right goods, in all the right proportions, in all the right places. No, she corrected herself, that was wrong—he had more than that. His goods weren't just right, they were better than that. He had the looks, the stature, the style. He was a walking enticement for the joys of love. And she was both woman and human.

With a soft moan and a shift of position, she huddled more deeply inside the jacket and tried to push Greg from her mind. She focused on a trio of school-girls wearing uniforms of multilayered denim and wondered what frivolity made them laugh. When they passed through the Commonwealth Avenue gate, she switched her focus to a pair of elderly men who occupied the bench across the pond. Their faces were tired and expressionless. She wanted to see them smile, and when they didn't, she looked away, skimming the garden until her gaze fell on a young couple necking against a tree.

Diandra watched them without compunction, reasoning that if they chose to air their kisses in public, they deserved to be watched. They were teenagers, the girl petite, the boy taller, and their bodies were bonded together as though they intended to stay that way for a good long time. The boy, who occupied the sheltered spot against the tree, had his wrists crossed over the small of his girlfriend's back; hers were wrapped around his waist. Their heads moved slowly, while their mouths remained fused.

Feeling a wave of distaste, Diandra looked away. She recalled similar waves of distaste she'd felt in the past when men had kissed her and she'd turned away. Then again, perhaps it wasn't distaste as much as disappointment she'd felt. She wasn't a virgin. She knew what to do. But mechanics were one thing, true pleasure another. Not finding the latter with either of the two men, who, in fourteen years, she'd cared for enough to sleep with, she'd pretty much given up on the former.

Her reaction to Greg was something else. Pleasure had been the last thing she'd expected to feel from his kiss, but feel it she had. She'd fought it and *still* she'd felt it.

Was it the necklace? Or was it Greg? Or was it some invisible quality, some chemical reaction that occurred between Greg and her the same way it had between their parents? Greg had always had the power to move her, but never before in this particular way.

She wondered if her mother had felt that all pervasive melting sensation, that mindlessness, that hunger in Greg, Sr.'s arms. If so, she could understand why she'd been seduced.

But only to a point. No woman had a right to hurt her husband that way. No woman had a right to hurt her daughter that way. And Diandra had been hurt. She'd lost her mother just when she'd needed her most, and there had been times when she'd been furious about that. Attraction or not, Abby should have been able to control herself. She had responsibilities. She should have put her husband and daughter ahead of whatever wayward feelings she'd had. She should have—and easily could have—put distance between herself and the source of temptation.

That was exactly what Diandra knew she should do herself. She should leave Greg in Boston and go home. But she couldn't do that. She was in a bind. For one thing, she'd told Bart she'd help him out, and she wasn't one to go back on her word. For another thing, there was San Francisco. More than ever, she wanted that store. It would give her a new cause, keep her busy, fill that void in her life that she increasingly felt. In San Francisco there would be new sights, new people. And what greater distance could she ask than that between east coast and west?

She raised her eyes to the sky. It was leaden, more so, perhaps, than when she'd started out. She wondered if it was going to rain and, thinking as a clothier would, wondered if she should dash home for the sake of the leather jacket.

Drawing one hand from a pocket, she fingered the fabric. It was a high-quality leather, the type Casey and York always carried in its most chic sportswear departments. It was cut in the standard bomber style that had been around for years and years. Still it seemed too big to have fitted Bart, even in his prime. She wondered whose it was.

Greg knew. Walking slowly back through the public garden after his swim, he took one look at Diandra sitting on that bench wearing that jacket, and the irony of it all—coming on the heels of what had happened earlier that afternoon at the town house—was too much.

The jacket had belonged to his father.

Coming to a halt, Greg dropped his gaze to the ground. He'd swum seventy-two lengths and had not only worked off the worst of his distress but also built up a pleasant fatigue. He was feeling calmer than he had, far more in control, nicely relaxed. He wasn't sure if he wanted to see Diandra just then.

He could turn around and take another path, he knew. Or he could continue on straight to the town house. Her eyes were downcast. She seemed lost in her thoughts. She wouldn't even know he'd passed.

But he'd never been a coward. And, besides, he *was* feeling calmer and more in control. He could handle himself.

With deliberate slowness, he started walking. He crossed over the bridge and turned onto the path that led to Diandra's bench. At the far end from where she sat, he stopped.

Startled by the intrusion of a human form nearby, she looked quickly up. As quickly, she recognized Greg and her alarm faded. Her heart wasn't as accommodating; it continued to pound.

Above his trim beard, his cheeks were ruddy. The wind had tossed his hair some in the drying. He was dressed as he'd been when he'd left except for a sweatshirt he thrown on over his shirt. The sweatshirt was faded and had obviously shrunk with repeated washing so that it reached a point just below his waist, which left plenty of room for his shirttails to show.

Although he wasn't exactly a fashion plate by Casey and York standards, he looked handsome in a disreputable kind of way. In sheer self-defense, Diandra tore her eyes from his to look intently out over the pond.

Greg studied her for a minute. She seemed very alone just then, not the sophisticated career woman he'd always thought her, but more approachable. He suspected that had something to do with the way she was huddled into the jacket, as though she needed protection. Seeing her that way, he doubted he'd have been able to turn around and leave her alone.

"Mind if I sit?" he asked.

Eyes still on the pond, she shrugged.

Taking care to leave plenty of room between them, Greg lowered himself to the bench. He set his ball of damp towel beside him and stretched out his legs. Not in the mood for an argument and not sure what to say that wouldn't cause one, he sat quietly.

Diandra wasn't sure what to make of his presence. Reluctant to deliberately court danger, she didn't look at him. But, oddly, she was relieved that he was there. She didn't know why it should be so, but the day didn't seem quite as chilly as it had moments before.

"How was your swim?" she asked.

"Nice."

"The pool was okay?"

"Not bad."

Nodding, she dropped her gaze to a scrawny squirrel that ran past. It looked as though it had just barely survived the winter. The ducks that swam past on the pond were in better condition. Of course, they'd been south.

"I loved that story," Greg mused quietly.

"Me too."

Make Way for the Ducklings had been an institution in Bart's home. No child who spent more than a day within the walls of the town house escaped a reading. Most children asked for seconds and thirds. Greg had. So had Diandra.

The ducks flew off, and across the pond a running child tripped and fell on the rambling root of a huge oak and began to cry.

Diandra sucked in a breath. Within seconds the child's mother arrived to soothe the wounds. Diandra released that breath.

Out of the corner of his eye, Greg watched her. The wind was blowing her hair around, so that he couldn't always see her face, but he'd seen the child fall, had heard her sharp intake of breath, and he was surprised. He hadn't pegged her as a woman who'd feel maternal instincts. Her own mother hadn't. Then again, maybe he was reading too much into her small gasp.

"Where's the necklace?" he asked.

She darted him a second's glance before homing in on the bridge, where foot traffic was picking up. "I'm wearing it."

A silent alarm went off in Greg's head. "That makes you mugging material."

"No one can see it. You're the only one who knows it's there. I'm not carrying a purse, and I don't have any other jewelry on. A mugger wouldn't look twice at me."

"Are you kidding?" he asked, raising his voice against all good intentions. "You don't have to be wearing jewels to attract attention. *Any* man would look twice at you just the way you are."

Diandra's lips twisted. "Funny, but that doesn't sound like a compliment," she said dryly.

"It's not. You shouldn't be walking around like bait."

"I'm not. I'm sitting. Quietly and unobtrusively."

"You shouldn't be alone."

"I'm not. You're here."

"I wasn't until a minute ago."

She did look at him down the length of the bench then, and said in a facetious tone, "If I didn't know better, I'd think you cared."

"Not quite," he replied, but his eyes held hers, and their warmth ignited an answering spark, which bounced back and forth, gaining heat with each turn.

Diandra was thinking that he looked rugged, not at all like the polished urbanite she'd always thought him to be. She was thinking that he looked good in jeans and shrunken sweatshirts and that, with his beard, he could have been a mountain man. There was something mysterious about mountain men. Something very masculine. Something silently appealing.

Greg was thinking that it had been a long time since he'd held a woman who fitted him as well as Diandra did. He was thinking that she had just enough height, just enough weight and that, with her hair blown awry and her cheeks pink and her face nearly naked, she was ripe for kissing. For holding. For making very thorough love to.

When he spoke again, his voice was a bit husky, a bit curious, a bit unsure. "Have you ever stopped to wonder what would happen if we didn't dislike each other so?"

Diandra was feeling the effect of his gaze from the top of her head to her toes. Heat seemed to be gathering in her chest. She had to swallow before she could speak. "No." She cleared her throat. "No, there's no point in wondering. We've always disliked each other. We always will."

"But we're attracted to each other," Greg said. He figured that they'd best get the problem out in the open since they were going to be working so closely together. "Do you deny it?"

She knew it would have been foolish to do so. He'd felt the response she'd made to his kiss. "I don't deny it."

"So?"

"So...what?"

"Can you handle it?"

She gave a sigh that was meant to sound bored. Unfortunately the effect was spoiled when it came out a shaky. "If you're asking whether I'm going to pounce on you and ravish you the minute we get back to the house, the answer is no. I can handle it, Greg. You're safe from me."

Greg wasn't so sure. Just the thought of Diandra pouncing on him had a provocative effect on his body—and that was before he'd even contemplated the ravishing part.

"Besides," she went on, needing to say something to give her argument force, "it's the necklace."

"What is?"

"The attraction between us."

Greg wasn't all that sure. "You really think so?"

She nodded, then looked away. She knew the necklace had *some* effect. Whether it was wholly responsible for the physical attraction was an interesting question. She wasn't sure if she was ready for the answer. "I think we have to keep busy," she said. She sought his eyes in earnest. "I think we should go back and get to work."

Having no better suggestion, Greg rose from the bench. Side by side, he and Diandra walked back to Charles Street, then up the hill to Bart's town house. They didn't talk. At no point did they touch. But they seemed to gain speed as they went, and by the time they were inside, they were ready to return to work.

With commendable resolve, they finished listing the contents of the living room. When they moved into the den, though, things got tougher. They both liked the den. The idea of dismantling it—and packing books was one of the few things they felt safe doing even before they'd contacted Bart—was distasteful.

Moreover, the room was small. Intimate. They were working side by side at the shelves, and it seemed that wherever one turned, the other was there. Very much there. And close.

Though the den held a wealth of memories for them, none of those was as vivid as the memory of that earlier kiss; Diandra and Greg were both thinking it. Each knew the *other* was thinking it. That knowledge made for awareness, awkwardness and tension.

Halfway through the second bookshelf, Diandra had had it. Dropping the pad of paper on the desk, she escaped to the wingback chair. Her skin felt warm, her limbs shaky. She was sure that Greg was purposely taunting her, purposely standing near, purposely stretching to reach books in a way that emphasized his height and strength. He was a beast, she decided. A large, lean, hairy beast. And she wanted to touch him.

Since she couldn't do that, she sat in the chair and glared at him.

He glared right back, but he didn't say a word. Instead, he moved behind the desk, picked up the phone and called New York.

Diandra knew he was trying the office. She knew because the very same thought had crossed her own mind not long before, when she'd been wanting a reminder of who she was and where she'd come from. But her timing, like Greg's, was off.

"No one's there," she informed him.

He turned his back on her and listened to the repeated ring of the phone that his private secretary should have answered.

"Greg, it's nearly seven o'clock at night," Diandra said impatiently. "No one's there."

He slammed the receiver down. "*We're* working. Why aren't they?"

"Because they've been working since eight-thirty this morning, while we've been piddling around, going swimming, taking walks—" she tossed a disgusted glance at the pad of paper "—making stupid lists." She turned beseeching eyes on him. "This is a monumental waste of effort. If Bart were here, he could tell us what he wants and what he doesn't, and what he wants done with what he doesn't want to keep."

Greg thrust his fingers through his hair, then rubbed the back of his neck. "We've been through this before, Diandra. Bart doesn't want to be here. That's why he sent *us*." Already, Greg regretted having agreed to come, and it wasn't only because he didn't like Diandra. Over the past few hours, he'd been tormented by the curve of her hip, the swell of her breast, the gloss of her hair, the graceful way she moved. He'd been tormented by the memory of how her body had felt against his, and he resented that. He needed to get out.

"But *anyone* can make lists," she was arguing.

Angrily he came around the desk and made for the door. Just beyond her chair, though, he changed his mind, turned back and put his hands on his hips. "Right. Anyone can. But Bart told us to do it." He paused and arched a tawny brow. "You want San Francisco?"

"Yes!"

"Well, so do I!"

"Then we should both leave. That'd solve the problem."

Greg held a hand toward the door. "Ladies before gentlemen."

She mimicked the gesture. "Age before beauty."

He didn't budge. "You go first. I dare you."

"Are you kidding? And let you stay here making dumb little lists? I'm not giving you San Francisco *that* easily." She squeezed her eyes shut, put her fists to either side of her head and said forcefully through gritted teeth, "This is the last thing I want to be doing with my life. I need a break. I'm tired. I'm hungry." Her eyes flew open when Greg grabbed one of her wrists and hauled her from the chair. "What are you *doing?*"

He was acting purely on impulse, as he'd rarely done before. "We're going out."

"Us? Together?" She pulled back on her hand and shook her head. "I don't think that's such a hot idea."

With a single tug, he pulled her against him. "You'd rather we stayed here?" he asked in a deep, vibrant voice. Still holding her wrist, he doubled her arm to her back. Though his grip was gentle, he held her firmly to his long, hard frame. "If you're looking for hot ideas, that's one." His eyes were dark and sensual, expressing everything they'd both been feeling being cooped up together for the past few hours.

Diandra didn't have to focus in on the warm hum in her veins to realize that his warning was worth heeding. Staying in the den—or anywhere in the town house, for that matter—wasn't the best of ideas just then.

"Out," she breathed. "We'll go out."

But suddenly Greg was having other ideas. The feel of Diandra against him was like heaven. "Then again," he drawled softly, "maybe we shouldn't. Maybe we should stay right here and see what happens."

"You don't want that," she said, looking nervously up at him. "You don't like me."

"True. But that doesn't mean it wouldn't be good between us."

When she tried to twist away, Greg circled her waist with his free arm, effectively locking her in.

"Let me go," she ordered.

Lowering his head, he put his mouth by her ear. "Is that what you really want?"

She closed her eyes. "Yes."

"Is it really?" he asked more hoarsely. "Come on, Diandra. The truth. Do you really want me to let you go, or should we explore whatever it is that's going on here." At the "here," he exerted a slight pressure at the small of her back. She felt it echo in her womb.

"It's the necklace," she cried. "That's all it is. The necklace is causing this . . . this . . ."

"Attraction? Need? Lust?"

"Yes!"

He held her back then, but only so that he could look at the necklace. For a long minute he was silent.

Then he said in a near whisper, "It really is beautiful."

"I'm going to take it off."

His eyes rose to hers, but his voice was the same
hushed sound it had been when he'd looked at the
necklace. "No. Don't do that."

"It's causing trouble."

He gave a short shake of his head. "It has a soothing effect. It kills the anger. It makes things better."

But Diandra couldn't see the necklace, so she wasn't
experiencing a soothing. Nor, though, was she feeling
anger. She was feeling…she was feeling Greg's broad
chest against her breasts, his tapering torso and muscular thighs supporting her softer frame. She was also
feeling his sex, firm and heavy, nestled snugly against
hers.

Her body felt hot and alive.

In desperation, she took her free hand from his
chest, where it had been holding him off, and touched
the gems. Her fingers slid over emeralds, skittered over
diamonds, traced gold. Filling her lungs with fresh air,
she felt the soothing, and she understood what Greg
had been trying to say. He'd been feeling anger, and
the necklace had blunted it. She'd been feeling acute
desire, and the necklace softened it.

Deepened it.

Enhanced it.

Aware of a trembling in her knees, she looked up at
Greg, but he was engrossed in the necklace. Releasing
her wrist, he brought his hand to her throat. He
touched an emerald, then a cluster of diamonds. Then,

using both hands, he gently eased open the collar of her shirt so that he could see the stones better.

Without his arms binding her, Diandra was free. She told herself to turn and run, but she couldn't. She could do nothing but hold her breath, because suddenly his fingers weren't touching the necklace. They were touching her skin. Very lightly. Very gently.

His eyes sought hers, capturing her in bounds of another sort and holding her while his fingertips skimmed her flesh. They brushed the tender skin beneath her jaw, slid down over her throat to a point just above the necklace, traced its outline. Then they skipped over the gems and continued the tracing, on the lower edge this time. That brought them under her shirt and around the back of her neck, then back over her shoulders and down, down to a point beneath the diamond fringe where her breasts formed a small cleavage.

With devastating slowness, he ran a single fingertip along first one gentle swell, then the other. And as if that weren't enough to set Diandra on fire, his coal-dark eyes smoldered with desire.

"Greg, stop," she whispered with mere remnants of breath.

"Let's make love," he whispered back. Wrapping one arm around her, he lowered his head and began to nuzzle her neck.

Diandra thought she'd faint. The feel of his beard against her skin was erotic in itself, but even beyond that, his mouth drove her wild. It moved moistly over the spot where her pulse beat a rapid tattoo.

Her legs felt like putty. Helplessly she shut her eyes and leaned into him for support, while her hands closed over fistfuls of his shirt. Driven by weak shreds of reason, she whimpered his name in protest.

Greg was more aroused than he'd been in months and months, but he wasn't so far gone that he didn't get her message. "Why not?" he asked in a voice that was muffled against her skin.

"Because..."

"That's not a good reason."

"Because... we're not... lovers."

"We could be," he coaxed. "Say the word and we could be. I want you, Diandra."

She could feel it. Lord, she could. He was richly aroused. "You'll regret it in the morning. *I'll* regret it in the morning."

"But do you want me now?" When she didn't answer, he held her back. When she refused to meet his gaze, he caught her chin and tipped up her face. "Do you want me?" he asked again. More so even than the dictate of his voice, the command of his eyes evoked her response.

"Yes!" she cried, then whispered, "I want you. But I won't make love with you."

Feeling the brunt of frustration, Greg took an unsteady breath. "Just because you don't like me? Since when does that matter?"

She stiffened. "What does that mean?"

"Come on, Diandra. You're not an innocent."

"I'm not sure I know what you're getting at."

"Your other lovers—was liking them a prerequisite to sex?"

The implicit accusation, coming from any other man at any other time, would have set her off like a bomb. But having been so aroused short moments before, Diandra was feeling vulnerable.

"Don't," she said, shaking her head.

"Don't what?"

"Make generalizations based on what you want to believe. You don't know me."

"I know more than you think."

"No." She pulled away from him and, wrapping her arms around her middle, moved out of reach. "You made certain judgments about my mother, and you're assuming the same things hold for me. But you were wrong about her, and you're wrong about me. You *don't* know me, Greg, and that's as good a reason as any for our not making love."

The hurt in her eyes was as clear as the pallor of her skin. Greg noted both and surprised himself by feeling remorse. He wasn't about to believe that she was a saint, any more than he'd ever believe it about her mother, but he didn't like that look of hurt. It bothered him—particularly knowing he'd put it there himself.

Bowing his head, he took several slow breaths. When he looked back up, he felt in control once more. Holding his head high, he said, "I think we're back to square one. I'm going out. Do you want to come, or would you rather stay here alone?"

As reluctant as Diandra was to go out with Greg, she was more reluctant to stay alone. She spent far too many nights alone as it was, and on this particular night, if her mind were idle it would have a field day. She needed to be occupied. She wanted a break. Since she wasn't about to go out on the town by herself, she guessed going with Greg was the lesser of the evils.

"I'll come."

Feeling an absurd sense of relief, he nodded and headed for the door, but Diandra wasn't moving so fast.

"Where to, Greg? I can't go anywhere fancy. I don't have the clothes."

He turned at the door and said, "Neither do I," which was ironic, given their occupations, but understandable, given the purpose of their trip. "I don't want fancy. I want casual and relaxed. Down to earth. Plebeian. I want to get something to eat. Walk around a little."

That all sounded comfortable to Diandra. And safe. "The Marketplace?"

He signaled his agreement with a small nod, then left to retrieve his sweatshirt. Soon after, he and Diandra were walking under the arches of the State House toward Faneuil Hall.

The Marketplace was perfect—just crowded enough, just loud enough, just busy enough. The atmosphere was positive and contagious. Diandra found herself relaxing. She didn't even mind when, guiding her one way or another, Greg put a light hand on her waist. The gesture was natural and nonthreatening.

For a time they went with the flow of the crowd, window-shopping, stopping to watch the street performers, ambling past one food booth after another. Unfortunately, when they decided to stop for dinner, it seemed that everyone else had the same idea. The restaurant lines were long. Greg, who'd been known to walk out of a restaurant when his reservation wasn't honored to the minute, wasn't in the mood to wait. So they did something neither of them had done in years and years. They returned to the food booths and picked up something here and something there, sharing most everything they bought, enjoying every last bite.

"Not the healthiest way to eat," Diandra remarked, using a paper napkin to wipe her hands of pizza grease. She'd already decided to avoid the bathroom scale the next morning.

Greg wasn't thinking about the scale as much as his doctor's warnings. He'd eaten several egg rolls, a chili dog, half of the taco that had been too hot for Diandra, and not one, not two, but three slices of pizza. "We'll live," he said in a droll tone, "and if we don't, at least we'll die happy." He steered her clear of a demon in a wheelchair and grinned. "There's something about eating junk food that boosts the spirits."

Diandra took his grin companionably. "I think it has to do with breaking the rules."

"Mmm. Our lives must be too structured. Too many formal dinners with rock cornish game hens—"

"And wild rice. Why always wild rice?"

"Beats me." As they ambled on, he looked down at her. "Are you tired?"

"No."

"Feel like going to Harvard Square?"

Her eyes lit up. "I haven't been there in ages."

"Me neither, but there's a bookstore that's open late—at least, it used to be open late. It could be we'd make the trip for nothing."

"Not that we have anything better to do," she reminded him.

"No," he said more quietly, then spread a hand on the back of the leather jacket and gently urged her out a side door of the arcade. "The Square is only ten minutes by T. If the bookstore's closed, something else will be open. We won't be bored."

The last thing on Diandra's mind was being bored. She felt extraordinarily relaxed and was having a good time. For the first time since she could remember, she didn't feel pressure either to look good or act properly executive or be witty or bright or intriguing. None of those things mattered. She knew people in Boston, but the chances were nil that those particular people would be walking these particular streets—let alone riding the T—at ten-thirty on a Tuesday night. And as for Greg, he didn't count. He didn't like her anyway, so it didn't matter what she said or did, or didn't say or do. As a result, she felt incredibly free.

Greg did, too, if the look of laid-back indulgence he wore was any indication. "I feel like I'm out on furlough," he said after they'd easily found seats on the half-empty train, which then began to rumble its way toward Cambridge. He grunted. "Strange that riding the subway should be a treat. That says something about one's life."

Diandra knew what he meant, but she wasn't in the mood to be philosophical. She was enjoying the rhythm of the train, the graffiti on the walls, the other passengers. "This place has character," she said with a grin.

Greg took in the grin. He took in the gentleness of her features, in such contrast to the "on" look she usually wore, and he wondered if she were truly enjoying herself, or simply too tired to be on. He'd never seen her quite that way, even at family gatherings. She always looked beautiful. Now she looked pretty, and there was a difference. He wondered if pretty was what turned him on.

They were sitting close beside each other, so he barely had to breathe for his voice to carry. "Where's the necklace?"

She patted the leather jacket where it snapped at her throat.

He nodded.

Leaning closer, she whispered, "It doesn't really have power, does it, Greg?"

Greg's eyes were on his and Diandra's reflection in the pitch-black of the train window. They looked for all the world like a couple very much involved with each other. "I don't know."

"Can an inanimate object have power?"

"I don't know as I'd call that thing inanimate. Whenever I look at it, it seems alive."

She shivered. "You make me feel like I'm wearing a snake." Repulsed by that thought, she turned to more whimsical ones. "We know that the necklace is old. We know from the inscription that it was originally given in love. Maybe the stones do have some mystical quality."

Greg was ready to believe most anything. Here he was, sitting beside his long-time enemy in a slightly decrepit subway car, heading for a late-night bookstore at an hour when he was most often at home studying spread sheets—and he was perfectly contented. Oh, yes, he was ready to believe something about those stones.

"We really should try Bart," Diandra said. She, too, saw the reflection in the glass, and though she knew she was probably sitting too close to Greg, she didn't move. She felt comfortable. Protected. Warm in all the right spots.

"There's more we can do by way of cataloging things before we need him."

She hesitated, then said, "About the necklace. Shouldn't we call him about the necklace?"

Greg mulled that over for a minute. "The way I see it," he decided, "Frederick was right. No one seems to be missing it, which means that Bart has to have been the one responsible for having it left on the mantel. Since he hasn't called to see if we've found it, why should we be concerned?"

There were any number of valid reasons why they should be concerned, Diandra knew, the major one being the sheer value of the piece. She also knew, though, that she didn't want to part with the necklace just yet. It did something; she knew it did. After all, she and Greg had been out together for several hours and neither of them had stormed off in a rage. Something had to be responsible for that.

Harvard Square was the same, yet not the same. The university spires were still there, as were the Coop and landmarks like the Out-of-Town News Agency and the Wursthaus, but redevelopers had been busy turning old brick buildings into chic minimalls. The stores and restaurants had definitely taken aim at yuppiedom.

The bookstore Greg had in mind was there, and open. They went in and browsed for better than an hour, moving from one rack to the next, one aisle to the next. Though they were often separated by books and people, if Diandra had been asked at any given moment where Greg was she'd have immediately been able to say.

And vice versa. In fact, Greg suspected he spent as much time looking between shelves at Diandra as he did thumbing through books.

When they finally left the store, they walked quietly back along Brattle Street. "Want some coffee?" he asked.

She smiled her thanks, but shook her head.

He looked down at her. "Tired?"

"Getting there."

"Should we take a cab back?"

She came to life then. "And spoil it all? No! I like being part of the masses." She wasn't ready to have the evening end. She wasn't ready to be confined in a small place with Greg. Just thinking of it was enough to stir sensitivities deep inside.

As it happened, though, the T ride back wasn't as carefree as the one out had been. The car was nearly empty, for one thing, which made for an intimacy of its own. For another thing, it was later at night than before, the time when sane folk were at home in bed, curled up in a lover's arms.

At least, that was what Greg was thinking. He'd always had an image of the way his life would be one day—coming home to an intimate dinner with his woman, spending quiet time with her, talking, laughing softly, going to bed together. If there was sex, great, if not, fine, because the important thing would be the closeness.

Thinking about that closeness now, he was confused, because he was feeling something like closeness to Diandra. And that couldn't be. He desired her. He didn't like her. She was too aggressive for his tastes, too contrary for comfort, too flighty where men were concerned. And sly. . . He knew that if he didn't watch out, she was more than capable of stealing San Francisco from under his nose.

Still, he felt that closeness. And desire.

It had to be the necklace.

Whatever its cause, he was thinking more and more about holding her as they emerged from the subway and walked back to the town house. She had her hands tucked safely in the pockets of the jacket, and her head was bowed, but the way she tossed him occasional glances, the way she pressed her lips together, then moistened them, the way she stayed close by his side suggested that she, too, felt the pull.

Opening the front door, Greg stood back and let her pass. She slipped out of the jacket and, when he took it from her hands to hang it up, murmured a soft thank-you. She didn't look at him, though, and by the time he was done she was halfway up the stairs.

"No good-night kiss?" he called in desperation.

She stopped on the stairs, bowed her head and said, "I don't think that'd be a good idea."

"Because you know it wouldn't stop there." He began the climb. "You know we'd end up in bed."

"We wouldn't. I wouldn't let us."

"Like you didn't let yourself respond to me before?"

When he came up behind her, she closed her eyes. She could feel his presence, feel it to her core. "Don't do this, Greg. It's been a nice night. Don't spoil it."

"I'm trying to make it even nicer."

She opened her eyes and turned to find him one step below her, which set them roughly at eye level with each other. While that didn't exactly give Diandra an advantage, it minimized Greg's. "No, you're not. You're trying to reduce the night to its lowest common denominator. Why can't you leave well enough alone?"

"Because I want you."

She shook her head. "Not good enough."

"You want me."

"Leave it, Greg."

"Just a kiss."

"No." She breathed out a sad sigh. "Kisses complicate things. I've got enough to handle without them." Turning, she continued on her way up the stairs, turned and climbed the second flight, then let herself into her room and shut the door.

If she'd yelled at him, called him a lecher, even told him he was a lousy kisser, Greg would have gone after her in a minute. But she'd been tired, sad and confused, and that had taken some of the punch out of the ache in his groin.

Actually the ache had moved to his stomach. He realized it when the last of desire faded, and he knew then that he was about to pay the piper for eating egg rolls, taco and pizza. He went to his room, took a healthy dose of antacid, then showered and went to bed knowing that if he was lucky the antacid would soothe the discomfort enough for him to sleep.

It wasn't his lucky night. He was still awake an hour later, and if the antacid had had any effect, he couldn't feel it. His punishment for disobedience was taking the form of real stomach pain—not intense enough to worry about, but strong enough to hurt.

He tossed and turned for a while, trying this position or that in search of a comfortable one. When he didn't find it, he got out of bed and tried walking around. When that didn't help, he went down to the kitchen, warmed a glass of milk, drank half of it as he wandered through the second-floor rooms, then returned to his bedroom and, propped up against the oak headboard, drank the rest.

It was there that Diandra found him a short time later. Used to the silence of living alone, she'd awoken when he'd first gone downstairs. She'd heard sounds coming from the kitchen, then silence, then the creak of the stairs, then silence again.

Something wasn't right. She felt odd. Holding a hand to the necklace, which in turn clung to her neck, she climbed from bed, crept to her door and, careful not to make a sound, opened it. Greg's room was around a corner, but even from her door she could see that his light was on. Walking softly, she went down the hall.

He was slouched against the headboard with two pillows bunched behind him, the sheet around his hips, one knee bent and an arm thrown over his eyes. All of him that showed above the sheet was bare, and she couldn't help but stare in appreciation.

His chest was beautiful. Large but not bulky, it was a canvas of tight muscle and lean flesh covered by swirls of tawny hair. His middle was a plane of sinewed ripples, his belly curved to accommodate his position. The tendons in his upper arm stood out in relief, as did the veins in his forearm. His fingers dangled limply.

She could have looked at him over and over again, but her gaze kept returning to those fingers. The Greg she knew was solid and strong, not limp. Something was wrong.

"Greg? Are you okay?"

His arm flew from his eyes. He held it in midair for a minute while he registered her sudden appearance.

Then, knowing that he was in no shape to properly appreciate the fact that she was wearing nothing but an old football jersey and the emerald necklace, he returned his arm to his eyes.

"I'm okay."

But she'd seen otherwise when he'd uncovered his face. He was pale and tired, and that alarmed her. "Aren't you feeling well?"

"Something I ate didn't sit right."

"I ate everything you did and I'm fine," she said gently, "so it couldn't be food poisoning."

"It's not."

She noticed the glass on the nightstand, noticed the white film of the milk that he must have drunk, noticed the roll of antacid tablets nearby. She looked again at his face, but between his beard and his arm, little was left to see.

Then he made a small movement, the tiniest shift of his middle, and she realized that he was truly uncomfortable.

"Is there anything I can do?"

"No. Thanks."

"Are you sure?"

"Uh-huh."

"Will you call me if it gets worse?"

"It won't."

Diandra wasn't sure whether that was sheer determination speaking or the voice of experience. She did know that it bothered her that he was sick, and that she felt inordinately helpless. She wasn't a Florence Nightingale. She didn't know what to do, and even if she had, Greg wasn't inviting her help. There wasn't much she could do but go back to bed.

"Well…good night, then," she murmured. "I'll see you in the morning." She lingered at his door for another minute, but when he didn't respond, she quietly left.

Back in her own bed, as she stared at the door she'd left open in case he called, she realized a second heavy truth of the day. Not only did she desire Greg, but somewhere inside her there was the capacity for feeling gentle toward him.

Either the necklace was truly to blame, or she was in trouble.

6

Diandra wasn't surprised when she slept until ten the next morning. She'd lain in bed for a long time the night before listening for sounds of distress in Greg's room, and when she finally fell asleep she slept lightly. Sometime about dawn she'd awakened and crept down the hall. His light was out, but enough of a haze crept in through the window to show that he was sleeping soundly. Only then did she do the same.

She would probably have slept even later than ten had it not been for the repeated peal of the door chimes. It took her a minute to remember that Frederick was gone, and then she jumped out of bed, grabbed the shirt she'd worn the day before and drew it on over her jersey. Barefoot, she ran down the two sets of stairs and peered through the peephole of the front door, only to sag against the door, then straighten and steel herself before opening it.

"Uncle Alex," she said, clutching the neckline of the shirt and trying to look dignified in a totally undignified outfit. "What a surprise!"

"The surprise was mine when I learned you were here," Alex said a bit archly as he plopped a perfunctory kiss on her cheek. Without pause, he stepped into the hall and closed the door, then gave her an admonishing once-over. "Not exactly the cream of our lingerie department."

She didn't have to return the look to know that her uncle was impeccably dressed. He was a handsome man, made even more handsome by his good taste in clothes. Standing before him now in an old football jersey and a wrinkled shirt, with her hair a mess, her legs showing from midthigh down and her face totally bare, she felt outclassed.

"I'm off duty," she explained.

"That's not what I heard. I heard you were here to close up this place for Bart," he mumbled under his breath. "The old goat. He knew he'd have to sell it quickly or I'd make a bid, and he couldn't bear the thought of that."

Diandra wasn't sure if she was ready for cold warfare first thing in the morning, so she changed the subject by asking, "How's Aunt Ellen?"

Mercifully Alex went with her lead. His voice returned to normal. "Just fine. She sends her love. Wonders whether you'll come to the house for dinner one night while you're here."

Diandra could think of any number of things she'd rather do. "Uh, I don't know if I'll have time. I'd like to clear things up and get back to Washington as soon as possible. Thank her for asking, though."

"Well, keep it in mind. The invitation's open." The words were barely out of his mouth when he raised his eyes.

Diandra turned to see Greg leave the staircase. He wore nothing but a pair of low-slung jeans, and with his hair ruffled and his eyes only half-open there was no doubt as to where he'd been moments before.

"How are you, Alex?" he asked in a sleep-roughened voice. Coming to stand by Diandra's shoulder, he offered his hand. Although he didn't care for Alex personally, he always tried to maintain the amicable professional relationship Bart had established.

"Not bad," Alex said, but his voice had a new edge to it. He looked at Diandra, openly disapproving. "When I heard that the two of you were here together, I thought I'd better come over to make sure one of you hadn't killed the other. It looks like I was worried about the wrong thing."

Only then did Diandra realize the picture she and Greg made. She opened her mouth to protest, but Greg beat her to it. His voice was suddenly clearer, deeper, more dangerous.

"That's quite a conclusion you've reached."

"Do you blame me?" Alex asked. "It's ten o'clock on a Wednesday morning, and the two of you look like you've just rolled out of bed."

Greg moved closer to Diandra. "We have."

"Separate beds," Diandra stressed, but she held her position. "I don't believe you, Uncle Alex. You know how I feel about Greg—*and* how he feels about me. What were you thinking?"

Alex stared at her in silence.

She'd seen him stare that way before, not at her but at her mother. Abby had taken it in stride, simply tossing her head and turning away. Diandra was nowhere near as calm. "Bart sent the two of us here to go through this place," she said tightly, "and it'd be pretty stupid for one of us to stay in a hotel. But believe me, neither of us wants to be here—together or at all." Resentful at having to make explanations, she raised her chin. "And even if something *were* going on, it wouldn't matter. I'm an adult. I can do what I want."

"True," Alex said grimly. "I just hope that when you do what you want, you know what you're doing."

"Always," she asserted, then set her jaw and waited for him to make the next move.

It was Greg, standing so close and bare that she felt the warmth of his skin through two layers of shirts, who tired of the standoff first. He ran a hand over his face and said, "It's too early in the morning for this. How about a rain check, Alex?"

Alex was standing stiffly. "No need. I just stopped by to say hello and to tell you that if there's anything you want while you're in town, you're to call."

"That's kind. Thank you."

Diandra remained silent.

With a final sharp look and a nod, Alex turned and left.

The instant the door was closed, she took off for the kitchen, where she angrily set to putting coffee on. By the time the beans had been ground and water was dripping through, she'd calmed down a bit. She turned to lean against the counter, then jumped when she saw Greg at the door.

The thought that he'd been watching her without her knowing it irked her. "Haven't you got anything better to do than to stand there gawking?"

"I'm not gawking."

"You're right. You're just standing there as calmly as you please." She pointed a finger toward the front door. "Didn't it bother you, what he said? He thought we were sleeping together!"

"So?"

"So we're not! But you know what's going to happen now, don't you? The grapevine will be humming."

"So?"

"So that's disgusting!"

Tucking his hands in the waistband of his jeans, Greg looked totally unconcerned. "Aren't you over-reacting a little?"

"No! There's no *way* I'd sleep with you. You are arrogant, selfish, competitive to the point of being ruthless, scrupulous only when it suits you and when it doesn't you're as unscrupulous as the next. On top of all that, you're a playboy."

Yet he stirred her. She didn't understand why, since he'd been a thorn in her side for as long as she could remember, but he did stir her. Wearing nothing but jeans—all long, trim, hair-spattered body—he was more man than she'd run into in thirty-two years. And it was a waste, since they were destined to be rivals.

"What grapevine have *you* been listening to?" he asked, but his back was turned before he finished, and she soon found herself alone.

With only the sounds of brewing coffee to break the silence, his words echoed in the air for a long time. *"What grapevine...what grapevine...what grapevine..."*

Only after she had returned to her room, showered and dressed, then come back to the kitchen for a second cup of coffee did she admit that he was right. She had listened to grapevines, so many that she couldn't begin to remember where and who. It seemed she'd been picking up little tidbits about Greg forever—not that she was obsessed, simply guarding her own interests. After all, her reasoning went, if she was to protect herself from Greg, she had to know what he was about.

So she'd listened to gossip, though she knew how unreliable it could be—and when it came to Greg, she wasn't objective to begin with. She heard what she wanted to hear, believed what she wanted to believe. If the truth were told, she didn't know much about him at all.

And that, she realized, was something to remedy.

Pouring him a cup of coffee—and making it light, then lighter still when she thought about the night before—she carried it along with her own into the den. Having tossed on a sweatshirt since their last encounter, Greg was sitting on the floor holding a small book. He set it aside when she approached and eyed first her then the mug with caution.

She held it out as an olive branch. When, after what seemed an endless minute, he reached up and took it, she breathed a little more freely. Sinking into the chair, she laid her head back and said, "You were right. I overreacted when Alex was here. He gets to me sometimes."

"I'd have thought you and he would be close."

"Because he was my mother's twin?" She shook her head. "Except for looks, they were very different. She had more energy, more flair. She overshadowed him, and he resented that. So he took delight in putting her down—though I'm not sure he understood what he was doing and why. I'm not sure it was a conscious thing at all." She averted her eyes. "They say blood runs thicker than water, but even when things started falling apart, he wasn't supportive. I don't think he knew how much that hurt." She frowned and added in a grim voice, "Then again, maybe he did."

Greg suddenly wondered who had hurt more— Abby, or her sixteen-year-old daughter. If Diandra was telling the truth about Alex's criticism of Abby, Greg could understand why Diandra had reacted so strongly to his accusation. It had hit too close. She felt history was repeating itself.

Greg knew for a fact that the present accusation was unfounded. Not that he wouldn't change that. He still wanted Diandra. She was all the more appealing sitting in her chair looking a little bruised. Though he'd never seen himself as a healer, he could think of a number of enticing ways to soothe her.

That is, assuming she was legitimately bruised and not just acting the part. He wasn't sure how far to trust her. Old habits died hard.

Unaware of the dark turn of his thoughts, Diandra was still thinking about Alex. "He didn't ask about the necklace."

Greg shifted his gaze from her face to the jewels and felt the incredible instant lightening that he was coming to expect. "He must not have seen it under your things."

She fingered an emerald. "But if he'd known about it—*anything* about it—he'd have asked. And he didn't. He didn't look guilty or suspicious or even curious."

They both sat quietly for a minute. Then Greg sighed. "It was Bart. It had to have been Bart."

"But what would he be doing with a necklace like this? Why would he have let someone leave it out on the mantel? I'm sure there are plenty of other jewels in his vault. Why isn't the necklace with them?"

Greg shrugged. "Maybe he thought he'd give us a thrill. It's a magnificent piece. Maybe he wanted us to see it for the sheer appreciation of it. Beneath all his bluff, Bart is a sentimental guy. Maybe he's a romantic, too."

She chuckled. "Anyone who makes *Make Way for the Ducklings* required reading for guests *has* to be a romantic." She focused in on the small book that Greg was picking up again. "What's that?"

He held it in his lap. "A book of poems. It's very old. He inscribed it to Emma, but from the notes in the margins it looks like he's been through it many times himself. I found it in the desk when I was looking for a pen."

"Poems?" She smiled and added on a note of surprise, "That's really sweet."

Greg had thought so, too, even though he knew more about Bart than most. "Most people think of him as a very organized, very shrewd, very efficient businessman. They'd never imagine that he was a packrat at home, but you wouldn't believe what he has hidden away behind these doors." He tossed his head toward the cabinets behind him.

Instantly curious, Diandra crossed to the cabinets, drew them open and dropped to her haunches to study their contents. Her eyes grew wider as she pulled out one bunch of papers, then another, then a pile of plastic bags filled with even more papers.

Lifting one of those plastic bags, she carefully reached in and withdrew the front pages of three separate newspapers, a handful of loose clippings and an assortment of handwritten letters. Selecting one at random, she read,

"Dear Bart, Just wanted to let you know how much we enjoyed ourselves at the party last Sunday. Juliet is a gem. It's hard to believe that she's just graduated from medical school. It must be even harder for you to believe that you have a granddaughter who is a doctor. You must be very proud. Enjoy her, and thanks again for including us in the festivities.

Most fondly,
Ethel and Brian Wright."

With growing amazement, Diandra quickly skimmed the newspapers, then the clippings. "These are the front pages of papers that were published on the day of Juliet's graduation."

Greg was looking through another plastic bag. "Same thing here, only this one's from the day of the christening of my cousin Tommy's first son, Bart's great-grandson. The invitation to the christening is here, several telegrams, the guest list."

Settling onto the floor, Diandra tugged out more bags. "He has them arranged chronologically, starting with recent events and working back." She flipped through. "Here's the big fund-raiser that was held in the Beverly Hills store eight years ago. And Joanna's wedding. And the grand opening in St. Louis." She looked up in time to see Greg take a shoe box from the bottom of the cabinet. "What's there?"

He removed the lid.

She caught a breath in delight. "Pictures? He saved pictures, too?" Shifting so that she was sitting flush to Greg's side, she looked on as he took out a handful of photos. They were old, black-and-white, faded to a misty brown. "These must have come from the original Kodak Brownie," she quipped, then asked, "Who is that?"

Greg studied the picture and turned it over, looking for identification on the back. There was none. "If I were to make a guess, I'd say the big guy is Bart's older brother, Henry Junior, and the little guy is Bart himself."

Entranced, Diandra pointed to a second picture. "And this one?"

"Bart's mother and aunt . . . or vice versa."

"Look at the clothes. Look at the car in the background. Look at the expressions! You'd think they were about to be shot."

"They were, euphemistically speaking."

Diandra laughed softly at that. "They look so sober." She urged his hand to the next picture. "I want to see more."

So did Greg. Studying one photo after another, he had a sense of history unraveling in his hand. Though there were many faces in the earliest pictures that they didn't recognize, Diandra was right—the clothes, the cars, the expressions were priceless.

Increasingly, as the time of the pictures advanced, they did recognize faces. Not only did they see aunts, uncles and cousins in younger days, but they saw their parents.

Two good-looking couples. A close foursome. Looking at the linked arms and smiling faces, they found it hard to believe that the future would hold what it did.

Less comfortable with those pictures than with the first, Greg slid a second shoe box from the cabinet. Balancing the box on his thigh, he let Diandra skim through. It didn't take her long to discover that they'd come upon the Thanksgiving pictures.

For as long as either of them could remember, it had been a tradition for the Caseys and the Yorks to celebrate Thanksgiving together. Diandra's grandfather had first started the custom soon after the store had begun to grow and the families had spread out; he'd wanted at least one reunion a year. When he'd died, Bart had faithfully carried on the practice.

At first, the gatherings had been held at one or another of the families' homes, and they'd been times of overall good cheer. After Diandra's mother and Greg's father had died, when there had been more tension between the clans, Bart had initiated the custom of gathering everyone on neutral ground for the long holiday weekend. They'd gone to Jamaica one year, Aruba another, St. Croix, St. Kitts, Guadaloupe and Martinique.... It had worked. Despite individual personality clashes, the vacation atmosphere had survived and the Thanksgiving tradition remained intact.

Diandra held up a picture taken on one of the more recent trips. "St. Bart's, three years ago." She smiled. "It was nice down there. Very French."

"Uh-huh."

Once she would have sent him a scathing look. Now she simply teased, "Don't sound so neutral. You spent the entire time on the beach, which just happened to be topless."

"I spent the entire time on the beach because I was exhausted and it was the only place I could get some rest. Your cousin had his six kids along. Once they discovered I could wiggle my ears, they wouldn't leave me alone. They drove me nuts."

"They're sweet kids—"

"When they're asleep." He pulled up another picture. "Santo Domingo."

"Ah, yes," she said wryly, "Santo Domingo. That was the year our reservations came through wrong and we ended up in a hole-in-the-wall where they had no idea what Thanksgiving was. Bart had to send home for turkey. It arrived the day after we left."

On impulse, she dug out a picture from the back of the box, took one look and gasped. "Look at us." There were at least twelve children in the shot, posed randomly on a cluster of rocks overlooking the sea. "I couldn't have been more than five." Her voice took on a humorous hush. "And you—without a beard."

"Without whiskers, period. Sorry to disappoint you," he drawled, "but I wasn't into puberty when I was ten."

At the sensuous note in his voice, her eyes flew to his. Only then did she realize how closely she was wrapped to his side. Subconsciously she'd gravitated to his warmth, and his body hadn't turned her away. She'd been comfortable, unaware of doing anything provocative or improper. Now, though, she started to straighten.

"Don't," he murmured, vaguely confused. He'd been enjoying the closeness. "It's okay."

Looking as confused as he, she gave a tiny shake of her head. It wasn't okay. It was too comfortable in ways that would lead to no good. She tried to remember whether her chin had touched his shoulder or her breast his arm, but the only recollection she had was of a general rightness.

Which puzzled her all the more.

With as little fanfare as possible, she slid to a safer spot against the open cabinet door, wrapped her arms around her bent knees and nodded toward the box.

Greg withdrew a new handful of pictures, thumbed through the first few, held up the third for her to see. "Remember that?"

"Sure. That was at my Aunt Helene's in Westchester." She studied the picture. "I was twelve."

"I was seventeen." He hissed out a soft breath. "Lord I was young."

"Young and randy. You were after everything in skirts—the maids, Uncle Herman's private secretary, even your own cousin's fiancée."

"I wasn't 'after' them," he argued innocently. "I was just being friendly. I was a senior in high school and feeling pretty important. All guys go through stages like that."

"You were flirting."

"You *thought* I was flirting because that was what you chose to see. I was being friendly. Period." He paused, then set off on a different tack. "And why not? I'd had to leave my own bunch of friends behind for the weekend, and I was into a heavy social phase. The family friends I wanted to see had managed to fink out on me—John was on an exchange program in France and Brice had just had an appendectomy. The adults thought I was a kid; the kids annoyed me. So I talked to the women in between.'' When Diandra rolled her eyes, he added an indignant ''I had to talk to *someone*. You wouldn't give me the time of day. You were as stuck-up as hell.''

She frowned. ''Stuck-up? I was never stuck-up.''

''You sure were.''

''You really thought that?''

He nodded. ''You stayed off by yourself—No, you were with your cousin Betsy most of the time, and she was so obnoxious that I steered clear. But even when you were with her, you were above it all, and when you were alone, you were *totally* unapproachable.''

Diandra was taken aback. She'd never thought herself unapproachable. True, she'd been guarded whenever Greg was around, because she'd been burned once too often. But unapproachable? Or stuck-up?

''I wasn't stuck-up. I was shy.''

He laughed. ''That's a good one.''

''I was,'' she insisted. She wanted him to know the truth. ''When I was twelve, when that picture was taken—and for several years after—I was *painfully* shy. I felt as though I wasn't anywhere near as bright or attractive as every other girl.'' She paused. ''Or woman.'' She paused again, then blurted out, ''My mother was vivacious. She was poised, witty, the life of every party. And she was beautiful. I wasn't. I lived in her shadow.''

Greg would have laughed at the absurdity of her claim had it not been for the earnestness of her expression. There was no doubt that she believed what she was saying. She might have been every bit as bright and attractive as every other girl, or as poised and witty as her mother, but she hadn't thought so. And that was what counted.

Uncomfortable with the compassion he felt, he tried to focus on a negative he did know about. Shuffling through several more pictures, he singled one out. "This was taken a year or two later. Look how you're standing, separate from the rest of us, looking angry. You were always snippy then. Perverse. You jumped at the slightest bait."

Diandra felt a dull ache as she studied the photograph. Oh, yes, she remembered. That dress. That vile dress. She'd had a huge argument with her mother over that dress. Abby had loved it. Diandra had hated it.

"If I ever have a daughter," Diandra vowed quietly, "I will be superattuned to her growing pains." Dropping her legs into a crossed position, she braced her hands on her thighs. "My fourteenth year was the pits. I wasn't smiling there—I never smiled—because I had braces and they looked ugly. Everyone else was getting theirs off, and I was getting mine on. That was because my teeth were two years behind my age—" she held up a hand "—but that wasn't surprising, since my *body* was two years behind, too. My friends had all developed, but I was totally flat. My mother said that my hair was adorable long and straight and pulled back with a ribbon, but I hated it. I wanted curls. And curves. I wanted to be pretty." She let out a breath. "I felt gauche. Out of it. I was constantly on the defensive."

Greg was surprised by her calm. "You were pretty then," he told her and meant it.

"I was not. I was backward."

"Was it so important that you look like your friends?"

She brushed her bangs from her brow with a forearm. "I've always been a competitor. I felt that I could do whatever I wanted—and be the best at it—if I tried hard enough." She frowned. "Puberty didn't respond to that kind of thinking. But the competitive angle tells only half the story. I didn't want to look like my friends, as much as I wanted to look like a woman. And yes, it was important. Identifying with a peer group is part of growing up. I was having trouble identifying with *any* group."

"Your parents couldn't help you over that rough stretch?"

She sputtered out a half-laugh. "My father thought I was just perfect the way I was. He adored me. He refused to hear that anything was wrong."

"And your mother?"

"My mother—" Her voice quavered, then steadied. "My mother was too busy to listen. If she wasn't having lunch with a friend, she was at a meeting of the hospital auxiliary or the garden club." Leaning forward, Diandra took the pictures from Greg's hand, flipped quickly through to a print she'd known would be there. Her hand shook slightly as she held it out. "I was fifteen when that was taken. Do you remember Thanksgiving of that year?''

Greg did. "We were at my aunt's place in South-ampton." He stared at the picture. "One year made a big difference. You looked like a woman there."

"Uh-huh," Diandra said tightly. "I had popped out, all right. All of a sudden, I found myself with the body I'd been dying to have, and I didn't know what in the devil to do with it." She nodded toward the pic-ture. "That Thanksgiving was probably the most miserable one of my life. I had gotten my period for the first time, the very first time. I had terrible cramps. I was terrified of going to the bathroom. And my mother was out somewhere with your father." Her voice fell to a whisper, as her anger dissolved into pain. "I needed her, and she wasn't there."

Feeling a desperate urge to move, she jumped up and crossed the room. She put her hand flat on a row of books, took a step back and looked down, then turned to lean back against the shelves with her arms wrapped around her middle.

"I'm sure it wasn't intentional on her part." She rushed the words out, trying to make up for sounding disloyal. "I'm sure she'd have been there if she'd known what I was feeling."

Greg wasn't so sure. He didn't credit Abby with having had anything in her character remotely related to self-sacrifice, which meant that if she was enjoying herself, she wouldn't have stopped for the world, let alone for her own daughter. He would have pointed that out to Diandra had she not been looking so upset.

Again he felt compassion for her, and again it unsettled him. To feel compassion was to be vulnerable. He feared that if Diandra suspected, she'd take advantage of him. So with little thought beyond shifting the focus of the discussion, he said, "You weren't the only one who suffered from that little affair. My mother was crushed. There hadn't ever been another man in her life. She adored my father. She lived to keep his home, raise his child, be the perfect hostess when he wanted to entertain, sit and hold his hand when he wanted quiet. The friends she had were his friends, and of those Abby was her *best* friend. Even at the end, when she learned what was going on, she blamed herself. Rather than yell and scream at my father or Abby, she withdrew into a corner and blamed herself."

He paused, remembering that time, feeling it again. "And I had to watch. I had to watch her in agony and know that nothing I could do or say would ease the pain. Not that I could have said or done much. I was crushed. My father had fallen from his pedestal. I was in my own kind of pain."

"But you were already a man," Diandra blurted out.

He didn't see the connection. "What's that got to do with anything?"

"You had graduated from college. You had just taken your own apartment."

"And I was supposed to be immune to it all?" Rising to his feet, he snorted as he went to the window behind the desk. Standing with his hands on his hips and his back to her, he said, "Sorry to disappoint you, sweetheart, but I was human."

She persisted. "You were a *man*. You'd already been through a dozen women and you hadn't settled down. Fidelity didn't mean much to you."

"A dozen women?" He turned to face her. "Sure, I'd dated a dozen women. I started dating when I was fifteen. Twelve different dates in seven years—not terribly decadent. But I never promised any of those women a thing, never swore undying love. And I didn't bed them all, you can be sure of that. Nor," he went on, nostrils flaring, "did my dad bed any other woman but my mom until Abby."

Diandra couldn't believe his naïveté. "Are you kidding? He fooled around for years."

"How do you know?"

"I know."

"How?"

"Everyone knew."

"Everyone but my mother and me?" Greg's eyes were as dark as pitch when he gave a slow, confident shake of his head. "My mother I could believe. She didn't have to look the other way because she was blinded by complete and utter trust. It never occurred to her to question that trust. I never had cause to suspect my father, either, but if there'd been cause I would have seen it before her. I'd seen parents of friends cheating on each other. I knew the signs. If my father had been fooling around before Abby, I'd have known it.''

His gaze narrowed on her in challenge. "So how did 'everyone' know my father had fooled around for years? Was he ever caught?"

"No, but—"

"Did any woman ever claim to have had an affair with him?"

"No, but—"

"Was there every any *concrete proof* that he'd been unfaithful to my mother?"

"It's next to impossible to get proof like that." Nervously Diandra fingered an emerald.

The movement of her hand drew his eye to the necklace. As he stared at it, the momentum of his argument broke, leaving a residue of hurt. He quieted. "We got proof of his affair with your mother. They were found together in the boathouse at Bar Harbor."

Diandra raised her eyes to the ceiling. "By your father's cousin, Angie. Good Lord, why Angie? She was the biggest mouth east of the Mississippi. Anyone else, and things would have broken more gently. Half the family knew about it before my father finally did."

"Or my mother."

"How could they have been so indiscreet?" Diandra cried. "Couldn't they have controlled themselves at least enough to go to some no-name motel where they wouldn't have been seen?"

"That's a damn good question," Greg said sadly. "And we'll never know the answer, will we? We'll never know why they took off in the plane that day, where they were headed, what they intended. We'll never know why the plane went down. We'll never know why they had the affair to begin with."

He looked at Diandra across the short distance separating them. Her face was as beautiful as ever, but her eyes held a pain that shouldn't have been there, and the injustice of it hit him.

They were victims. Both of them. In that instant of realization, Greg saw that none of the hostility that had come before mattered. All that mattered was that they were the victims of a tragedy that should never have been, and that they both suffered.

His steps were slow but sure, the kind that happened and were done without notice. Taking Diandra in his arms, he drew her close. She came willingly. Sliding her arms around his waist, she put her cheek to his shoulder and took the comfort she needed. And she did need that comfort. She hadn't ever before verbalized the feelings as she just had. They'd been buried beneath years of diversion, but Greg's goading had dredged them up, and they hurt.

She'd dredged something up in him, too, though, and it surprised her. It had never occurred to her to think of him as having been hurt by their parents' relationship. Angry, yes—at Abby, and her. But hurt? He'd been grown up, independent. She'd always assumed he was too arrogant to feel something as mundane as hurt. She'd never thought of him as feeling, period.

She'd been wrong. For all the comfort he was giving her now with the strength of his body and the warmth of his skin, he was taking a comfort of his own. She could feel it in the way his arms circled her and the way he bent his head to her neck. He held her as though she had something special to offer him— and as though he desperately needed that offering.

With a sigh, she tightened her arms. Holding him was like holding to a rock in a storm, but he was a rock that needed protection, too, and that made a difference in what she experienced. She was finding as much comfort in the giving of comfort as in the taking.

When he moved his mouth on her hair, she took a deep, satisfied breath. There was something very right about their holding each other, offering each other support for a pain they shared. She'd never thought Greg would be an ally in that particular respect.

Looking up, she found his eyes a clearer, softer gray than she'd ever seen them. They warmed his entire face and drew her to him all the more. Moving her arms higher on his back, she returned her head to his neck to find a spot just below his close beard that seemed made for her. She nestled there, feeling at home with the natural musk of his skin. And at peace. She was stunned by the incredible peace she felt, particularly coming as it did on the heels of inner turmoil.

Greg, too, felt the peace. He guessed that he could go on holding Diandra forever—she fitted in his arms that well. But it wasn't only a physical thing. It was a communing of minds. Odd that he should be able to do that with Diandra, of all people. They'd been at opposite ends of the spectrum for as long as he could remember, yet the spectrum seemed to have suddenly shrunk. At that moment, they were close.

The minute stretched from one to two, then three, and still the sense of rightness went on. If anything, it intensified, gaining in strength as the seconds ticked away.

Without pausing to think of the consequences, Greg lowered his head and kissed her cheek. It was the most natural thing in the world for him to do, the most honest way to express the closeness he felt just then. Apparently Diandra thought so, too, because she turned her head the smallest amount until her lips touched his.

Her kiss wasn't seductive. It wasn't coy or contrived, but gentle and sincere. It said, "Thank you" and "I needed that" and "I need this, too" with such simplicity that Greg would have had to have been the insensitive clod she'd accused him of being to miss the message. But he wasn't that clod, and her silent voice rang through to his senses. He kissed her with the same thanks she offered, marveled at the newness of it, returned the same gentleness—then was promptly hit by a wave of greater need.

That, too, was mutual. When his mouth grew more hungry, Diandra's kept pace. Her lips fell slack when he began to nibble on the lower one, but by the time he was back to a full kiss, she was returning it in kind.

Her arms were wrapped tightly around him, her body pressed close.

In the end, he was the one to draw back and look down into her flushed face. Her lips were moist and parted. Her eyes were dazed, but several seconds of his scrutiny gave them a confused look.

Greg needed that look as much as he'd needed the kiss. If she was confused, it meant that her response to his kiss was unpremeditated. That mattered.

"What's wrong?" she whispered, disoriented.

In that instant, he felt true affection for her. "You don't know what you're doing," he murmured gently.

She shook her head to clear it and frowned. "I . . . no."

"We'd better stop."

Her eyes registered a faint protest. Disorientation notwithstanding, she knew that something felt very good and that she didn't want it to end.

His whisper was rough, yet gentle still, his breath warm on her face. "This is getting out of hand."

"We were only kissing. It was nice."

She said it so innocently that he couldn't find it in himself to be angry. "But I want more," he said quietly. Sliding a hand between their bodies, he ran his knuckles against the outer swell of her breast. "I want to touch you. Undress you." His eyes held hers while those knuckles passed with ghostly lightness over her nipple, which quickly hardened. "I want to see you naked," he added in a husky whisper.

Between his words, the brush of his hand, the dark sensuality of his eyes and the intimate pressure of his body, she was being assaulted on all sides. In an attempt to cut down on that sensory input, she closed her eyes, but that only enhanced her awareness of Greg. Or was it that he chose that moment to open his hand on her breast? Or that his arousal was becoming more pronounced against her belly?

A soft sound came from her throat, followed by a gruffer sound from Greg that brought her eyes open in a flash.

"You're no help," he muttered. "No help at all." Hands on her shoulders, he held her at arms' length. "Tell me you don't want to make love."

"I don't want to make love," Diandra echoed, knowing that despite the clamoring of her body it was the right thing to say.

"With conviction. Say it with conviction."

That took more doing, but she managed, if for no other reason than to prove to Greg that she wasn't the seducer. Given whose daughter she was, that was very important. "I don't want to make love," she said firmly.

Greg studied her face. He wasn't sure whether he was pleased or not that she'd done as he'd asked. He was still hard. There was only one antidote.

"Then let's get to work," he said. Releasing her, he turned away before he could change his mind.

7

Diandra and Greg spent the rest of that day listing the books in the den, grouping them by category, packing them into well-marked cartons. It was an unpleasant task. With each shelf that was bared came a sense of loss. Working quickly helped. The more intense their participation, the less they could dwell on what had happened between them earlier. Neither wanted to analyze the kiss, the embrace, the words of need they'd exchanged. Analysis would invite criticism—of themselves and each other, if for no other reason than the force of habit—and those moments had been too special for that. It seemed best to leave well enough alone.

Unfortunately as the afternoon passed Diandra discovered that well enough wasn't satisfied with being left alone. The den was too small. Greg was too large. The task was too demanding of closeness to allow for breathing space. They seemed to be forever knocking arms or elbows, and she was aware of every touch. Her heartbeat echoed each. Her internal thermostat ran warmer than usual. It was as though, once turned on, the current of awareness defied detour.

More than once she put her hand to the emerald necklace in search of a balm, and she did get it, but not in quite the way she'd sought. The necklace calmed her. It made her feel as though, in the long run, things would be fine. It painted the world a little brighter.

But it did nothing to still the deep, throbbing reaction she had to Greg, and that reaction was triggered each time he came near. Her only hope against it was to work harder, which was what she did.

So did Greg. As he'd done the day before in the pool, he chipped away at sexual tension by pushing his body in another direction. Strangely he had an easier time of it precisely because Diandra was there. He was competitive; so was she. Though they divided the labor to maximize output, with one feeding books from the shelves to the other to pack, they kept each other working steadily. By the time late afternoon rolled around and the last of the books had been packed, they were understandably tired.

Standing into a stretch with her hands massaging the tired muscles of her lower back, Diandra looked around the room she'd once loved. It was no longer the same cozy haven, but had become something barren, not familiar at all.

"This is depressing," she announced.

Greg agreed. He'd tried not to notice the thrust of her breasts against her shirt when she'd stretched, but he'd noticed anyway, and his body—which was supposed to be worn out—had quickly tightened. Scowling for more reasons than one, he eyed a particularly high stack of cartons. "Bart better know what he wants done with these. I sure as hell don't."

"Me neither." She sank back against the desk, then, almost immediately rethought the move, pushed off and made for the door.

Moments later, Greg found her sitting on the bottom stair in the hall. One palm cupped her chin. The fingers of the other hand touched the necklace. Even in spite of the smooth grace of the emeralds, she was looking as upended as he felt. On impulse, he lowered himself to the stair beside her.

Diandra rolled her eyes.

"What's wrong?" he asked.

"I don't believe this. With an entire houseful of seats to choose from, you choose mine."

"I didn't see your name on this step."

"No, but my bottom's here."

He turned his head to slide a glance down her back to the item in question. "It's small enough. We fit."

She made the mistake of returning the glance. Thanks to the way he was sitting, leaning forward with his elbows propped on his knees, the ribbing of his sweatshirt didn't quite reach his jeans. In between was an inviting strip of firm flesh, slightly indented on either side as it approached the small of his back. Millimeters above his jeans was a thin white line that could only be his briefs.

"That's the problem," she murmured weakly.

Greg stared at his hands, then sent her a sidelong glance. "Getting to you, too, is it? Maybe if we move right on to another room and attack it the way we did the den, we'll wear ourselves out. If we work our-selves ragged, we won't have the strength, and that will be that."

Diandra wondered. She was beginning to think the attraction she felt for Greg was predestined. "The way I see it, it's either something we inherited from our parents... or it's coming from the necklace. There's no way you and I can want each other on our own."

"Because we hate each other."

"Right."

Focusing on the mahogany console across the hall, Greg idly gnawed on the inside of his cheek. He didn't hate Diandra. He always had—or thought he had—but he didn't feel it now. She could still annoy him, but there had been times in the past forty-eight hours when he'd thought her amusing, even sweet. What he'd once considered impulsiveness now seemed more like spontaneity—and he found that surprisingly refresh-ing.

Yes, there were moments when he liked her, and the small voice inside that told him to be wary was grow-ing softer and softer. She seemed genuine, strangely genuine....

He shot her a glance. She was studying the floor, but at the movement from him she met his gaze.

"Ever been in love?" he asked with deliberate lightness.

She shook her head.

"Me neither."

"Ever missed it?" she asked back.

He shrugged. "How would I know what to miss if I've never felt it?"

"You'd know. You'd see it in other people. You'd look around at friends and see something you wish you had. You'd feel a void."

"Do you?"

Tearing her gaze from his, she moved her fingertips over a diamond cluster as though it were braille. Then she looked back at him and nodded. "Sometimes."

"You want a husband?"

"Sometimes."

"And kids?"

"Sometimes."

"Sometimes doesn't work when it comes to those things."

"Maybe that's why I don't have them. I've never been willing to make the commitment. I've been too busy building a career to allow the time for it."

"Has it been worth it?"

"I love my work."

"But has it been worth it?"

Diandra was frustrated. She wanted to give him an honest answer, but she wasn't sure she could. Dropping her hand, she dragged both palms along her thighs, back and forth, and said, "It's not fair. Modern society tells a woman to work. It doesn't recognize her as legitimate unless she brings home a paycheck, but if she does that, where is she supposed to find time for a husband and children?"

"Many women do it."

"Not ones who do what I do." She held up a hand. "I'm not complaining. Like I said, I love my work. And the fact is that I'd probably be as busy in any job I held, just because that's my nature. I like to do things well or not at all." She frowned then, and her voice shrank to a discouraged murmur. "I suppose that would apply to a husband and kids. I don't think I could do them justice if I tried to juggle them around CayCorp, and I'm not ready to give up CayCorp."

He studied her face. She seemed legitimately disturbed, but so was he. He was trying to figure her out, trying to somehow reconcile the different images he had of her. "So that's why you've never married?"

"I've never married because I've never been in love."

"Then love is the key? You'd give up CayCorp if you fell in love?"

"I didn't say that."

"But you would marry if you fell in love?"

"I don't *know*. I couldn't ever marry without being in love, but I could be in love without getting married. It would all depend on who and where and what the man I loved was."

"This is getting complicated."

"I know."

"But it shouldn't be. You've dated some illustrious people, had your choice of the best of the bunch, and nothing's clicked. Is CayCorp that tough a competitor? What is it you want from the business anyway? Are you aiming to be president one day? Chairman of the board?"

His tone wasn't harsh. It was conversational, curious. But his words touched a sensitive chord in Diandra. Stung by what smacked very much of the old Greg just when she was letting down her guard and opening up, she started to rise.

He grabbed her hand. "Whoa. I asked a simple question."

"You asked a bunch of questions, each one loaded." Her eyes were wide and confused. "How in the world should I know what I'm aiming to be? I'm too busy being what I *am* to aim further just now. That's the whole point of what I was saying, which you would have seen if you hadn't been trying to trip me up. I'm not ruthlessly ambitious. I'm not trying to steal either the presidency or the chairmanship of the board from you."

"You're trying to steal San Francisco," he said without thinking.

"Not steal, since you don't have it to begin with, but I'm convinced that I'm the best one for the job." She paused. "And just to set the record straight, I haven't dated any particularly illustrious men—nor do I care to. Illustrious men have illustrious egos. I don't have the time for men like that."

"So who do you date?"

"Not much of anyone." She glared at her wrist, what little of it she could see between his fingers. "Do you mind?"

"Yes." He gave a gentle tug. "Sit down again. I like it when your bottom's next to mine."

Pressing the heel of her free hand to her forehead, Diandra closed her eyes and sighed. "I wish you wouldn't say things like that."

"I won't say things like that if you'll sit down. Why do you always have to be so prickly?"

"Because you prod and prod until you pierce the skin and get underneath." Her eyes opened and went straight to his. "It hurts sometimes, Greg. Why can't you see that?"

He asked himself the same question as he studied her look of pain, and there seemed only one valid answer. "Maybe because I'm not used to seeing this side of you." His fingers gentled on her wrist, and he gave a lighter tug this time before releasing her entirely.

After a moment's pause—during which Diandra realized that she liked her bottom next to Greg's, too—she sank back to the step. Tucking her hands between her knees, she pressed them together.

"So," Greg said. "What next?"

"I don't know."

"Want to attack the dining room?"

"To eat or pack?"

"Pack."

"Not really."

"Eat?"

Without looking at him, she tipped her head and said in a musing tone, "I could use a little something."

"I could use a *lot* of something."

She did look at him then and found something terribly endearing on his face. With a will of its own, a small smile crept to her lips. "Spoken like a man who hasn't eaten in days."

He shook his head. "Spoken like a man who hasn't eaten since lunch and who's done hard physical labor ever since." His eyes narrowed. "I feel like a good, thick, juicy steak. Think Frederick has any good, thick, juicy steaks in the freezer?"

She turned up her nose. "You don't want frozen. You want fresh."

"I'd take anything right about now."

"Like tacos? Or pizza?"

"Uh . . . almost anything."

She'd been teasing him with her reminder of the trouble he'd had the night before, but with his qualification, her grin faded. "It's an ulcer, isn't it?" she asked softly.

Greg's eyes shot to hers, his guard instantly up. If she thought she'd use health as an argument against his getting San Francisco, she had another think coming. If need be, he would deny that he suffered anything more than indigestion.

But her voice was gentle, her eyes concerned, and the two combined to touch something deep inside him.

He gave a one-shouldered shrug. "A small one. Nothing that can't be controlled with sane eating."

"And we overdid it last night."

"*I* overdid it," he corrected, putting blame where blame was due. "I'm usually pretty careful. But it was fun last night."

She agreed with that, though she wondered, "Was the pain worth it?"

"Yes," he answered instantly. Even after he thought about it, he repeated, "Yes. My life is too controlled, everything orderly, structured, programmed. If the ulcer came from tension, I can't think of a better way to counter it than to relax and enjoy myself, and that's exactly what I did last night." He looked at her, almost defying her to say he'd been wrong.

"It's okay," she said quietly, then tacked on, "as long as you don't binge on fried foods every night. How will steak sit?"

He breathed more freely. "Great."

"Where can we get it?"

"The Chart House. It's on the waterfront."

Diandra dropped a despairing look at the shirt and jeans she wore, than at the sweatshirt and jeans on Greg. "Will they let us in?" she asked.

"Not like this." He glanced at his watch. "But we still have time."

Her face brightened. Then she broke into a smile. "Not a bad idea." Using his thigh as a prop, she pushed up from the stair. "Not a bad idea at all." Her smile grew impish. "We could do it dressy—full length, black tie and tails." When he wrinkled his nose at that suggestion, she asked, "How about city suave?"

"Maybe," he said, rising and starting up the stairs. "Or country club chic." He ran a palm across his chest. "I need a shower first. Feel really grubby."

"Hurry," she called after him. "The store closes at six."

Grubby or not, Greg was feeling incredibly buoyant. "We *are* the store," he declared. "It'll open for us whenever."

They arrived at Copley Place at five forty-five so Casey and York didn't have to open specially for them. To their mutual relief—which they joked about—Alex wasn't there to mark their less-than-noteworthy entrance. He had gone for the day, leaving a bevy of managers to supervise the store's closing.

For those fifteen minutes until closing time, Diandra and Greg wandered through the store with total anonymity. Though each had been there before, neither had been there at leisure. They wandered from department to department observing layout, admiring displays, noting the way the salespeople dealt with customers—and comparing all those things with their own respective stores.

In spite of whatever other faults either of them found in Alex, they agreed that he was an effective administrator. The store was elegant, as befitted its location, and appeared to be well run. Although certain departments were played up or down in variance from their treatment in either New York or Washington, the merchandising was tailor-made for Boston.

Busman's holiday over, they identified themselves to floor managers and parted ways to choose clothes for the evening. Twenty minutes later, as prearranged, they met at the foot of the first floor escalator.

Diandra wore a silk jumpsuit with padded shoulders and a nipped-in waist. Buttons ran down the front, but she had them fastened high to conceal the emerald necklace. The corners of her collar crossed stylishly beneath her chin. A cardigan sweater-coat was draped over her shoulders. The coordinated mauve of both silk and knit played up the creamy hue of her skin and the raven blackness of her hair.

Greg wore a pair of gabardine pants, an open-neck silk shirt and a free-fitting tweed blazer. He looked very tall, very cosmopolitan, very dashing. The color of his shirt was nearly identical to that of Diandra's jumpsuit.

"Great minds think alike," she mused, noting that mauve made Greg look that much more tawny, even more striking than usual.

Greg didn't say a word at first. He couldn't take his eyes off her—off the gracefulness of her neck as her collar framed it, the swell of her breasts beneath silk, the lengthy look of her legs made even more so by slender high heels, and the soft flush on her cheeks. He wondered if dressing up had been such a good idea after all. He'd seen Diandra dressed up before. Never before had she done it for him, though, and that made a difference.

"I hope," he began, then cleared his throat and began again, "I hope we won't be taken for a couple of grapes."

She laughed at that, then said, "You look great." She stood with the Casey and York bag that held her old clothes dangling from her linked hands.

"So do you." He reached for her bag and tucked it into his own, which he then slung over his shoulder. "All set?"

She nodded.

"Hungry?"

She nodded more vigorously.

Without another word they left the store and hailed a cab for the waterfront.

The Chart House came through with two of the thickest, juiciest steaks they'd ever eaten, but the focus of the meal wasn't the food or the service or the harbor view. It was each other. Though they'd known each other since childhood, though their jobs overlapped and they saw each other often, they had never before sat down together at a restaurant, just the two of them for several hours of private conversation.

They discussed a wide range of neutral topics—mutual acquaintances, *Les Miserables*, the stock market. They exchanged tidbits of CayCorp gossip, then went on to discuss the advertising campaign that so worried Bart.

Diandra found that when he wasn't looking to zing her, Greg was the most interesting companion she'd had in years. He was intelligent and responsive, and though she'd always focused on their differences, she had to admit that they had a great deal in common.

The man who had been her nemesis seemed a world away. In his place was an eminently likable man. He asked questions without goading. He expressed his opinions without putting hers down. He seemed to have set aside enmity for the sake of the evening.

She wondered whether it was the wine they drank that sweetened his mood—and hers. She did feel sweeter. More relaxed, less guarded, less defensive. The mellowing hadn't been a deliberate thing, but had just happened, and it was self-perpetuating. Diandra hadn't enjoyed herself as much in a long, long time. She wanted to prolong that.

It helped that neither of them mentioned either San Francisco or their parents.

And it helped that she was wearing the necklace. Though hidden beneath her collar, it was a living presence against her skin. Like a talisman, it gave her confidence—both that she could hold her own with Greg and that being with him was right. It told her not to look to the past or future, but simply to enjoy the present, which was very much what she was doing.

By the time they reached dessert, they were constantly smiling. Between them, they had drained a full bottle of wine though Greg, for one, couldn't blame his light-headedness on that. He rarely got tipsy. Besides, he was feeling as lighthearted as he was light-headed, and he'd never had that particular reaction to wine. Not that he would have minded. Either light-headed or lighthearted was preferable to horny.

By mutual consent, when neither of them wanted dessert, they set off on foot for Beacon Hill. The exercise was welcome after the meal, and the chill in the air was just the thing to cure light-headedness—or so they reasoned.

That didn't prove to be the case. As they walked along at a jaunty pace with their elbows linked, they found one amusing tale after another to share. They laughed loudly and often, uncaring if passersby stared at their unbridled exuberance, which only gave them something else to laugh about once that particular passerby had passed by. They'd never in their adult lives been silly that way; they felt they were taking their due.

After cavorting their way through Government Center, they passed a video rental store that catered to night owls. Greg promptly dragged her inside and insisted they rent a movie to play on Bart's VCR. From shelf to shelf they went, bickering good-naturedly about what choice to make. They studiously avoided those shelves with anything sexy, and when they finally checked out a newly released adventure film, they felt they'd made a safe choice.

So they returned to the town house, where they changed back into jeans for the sake of lounging more comfortably in front of the TV. The scene called for popcorn but they were too full to eat so they opened another bottle of wine. Then, sitting side by side on the floor with their backs against the sofa and every light in the room off, they proceeded to joke their way through the first half of a movie that, on any other occasion, would have been a thriller.

They didn't quite get involved in the plot. First Greg found that he could announce what was going to happen before it happened, then Diandra found that she could speak the dialogue before the characters did. They toasted themselves each time they were right, and they were right often enough to keep the wine flowing, which meant that they felt little pain when they were wrong.

In time, though, Diandra grew sleepy. Dropping her head to Greg's lap, she closed her eyes and was out within minutes. Too bleary-eyed to fully appreciate her position, Greg pulled pillows from the sofa, propped them under his head and was soon asleep himself. The movie ended with neither of them observing its climax. The set automatically shut itself off, filling the dark room with silence.

Greg was the first to stir. He'd been having an X-rated dream, and when he tried to shift position, he discovered the object of his dream in the flesh. Her head was no longer in his lap, since he'd stretched out earlier, but she was curled close to him with one arm across her chest and the other over his hip.

Eyes closed, he nuzzled her hair. Its scent and her warmth were extensions of his dream, so pleasant that he made no attempt to wake himself further. He brought a hand lightly through the silky mass, then bent his head lower and kissed her ear.

She moved. Just her head. Just enough to give his mouth better access. Still mostly asleep, she reacted instinctively to the gentleness of his lips and his warmth by gravitating toward both. It was her silent way of saying Mmm. I like that. It's nice.

As though he'd heard her, Greg drew a line of slow, moist kisses from her ear to her cheek. He liked the smoothness of her skin and its fresh smell, liked the idea that he didn't have to kiss his way through layers of makeup to reach the woman beneath. Diandra was pure in that sense. Though he couldn't see her in the dark, he knew the exact shade of that creamy skin. She was inviting, far more so than any woman he'd ever had or dreamed of having.

Needing to deepen the contact and prove it real, he slid his fingers into her hair to hold her while his lips covered hers. She tasted faintly of wine, faintly tart, faintly sweet. And he was suddenly more thirsty than he'd been seconds before. Caressing her lips apart, he slid his tongue into her mouth.

Diandra came awake with a muted gasp. Instinctively her hands rose, one to his chest, one to his shoulder. Her palms were against him, prepared to push him away. Her fingers were straight in surprise, but with the sensual stroking of his tongue, they closed around handfuls of his shirt and clung.

The kiss went on and on, deepening by increments until Diandra was as active and involved as Greg. All remnants of sleep had gone, but still there was something dreamlike about that mating of mouths. It was very new, very exciting. It was simultaneously the most satisfying and frustrating experience of her life.

Destiny. That was the one word that came to Diandra's mind as she slid her hands over Greg's shoulders and arched closer. She felt as though she'd arrived at a spot that had been preordained years before, and though that spot was hot with desire and far from peaceful, she felt she was home.

Greg, too, felt the homecoming, but on a far less cerebral level than Diandra. His body was tight, clamoring for a satisfaction only she could offer, and with each kiss, that need grew. Never before had he felt such a desperate need to be part of a woman. He'd always thought himself too self-contained, too self-controlled, too independent for that, but Diandra was proving him wrong. He felt less than whole; she was the only one who could complete him.

Sliding an arm around her, he brought her hard against his body. When even that pressure wasn't enough, he rolled over until he half-covered her and thrust against her heat.

The strength of his arousal was stunning. Diandra arched upward. While her hands found a hold in his hair, her hips began a slow undulation that harmonized with his, and the breath she was holding gradually found its escape through soft moans of desire.

To Greg, each moan was a promise. Each one painted a picture of their bodies, entwined as they were, but naked. The moan then was his, and no sooner was it out when he sat up on his knees, drew Diandra with him and settled her between his thighs.

He touched her everywhere. His hands made a statement of possession that was less than gentle at times, but always arousing. Her clothes didn't deter him. He greedily claimed her shoulders, her back, her breasts and belly, and as much as he touched her, she strained for more. Bombarded with sensation, she entered a state of overload where the only thing she felt was an incredible, searing heat. When he cupped her bottom and drew her to him hard, she bit her lip to keep from crying out. When his hand found its way beneath her to the greatest point of her need, she thought she'd die of want.

Trembling from the inside out, she made a small, strangled sound, but her thighs parted to accommodate him, leaving no doubt as to the meaning of the sound.

Of one mind as to their destination, they hurried. Between soft, shuddering breaths, they pulled at snaps and zippers, tugged at denim, kicked unwanted clothes aside. They barely had time to unbutton their shirts when the urgency of the moment took them. Diandra lay back on the carpet, Greg followed her and was inside with one, long thrust.

She cried out. As ready as she was for him, her body was tight. His sudden invasion, his sheer physical presence inside, startled her. She dug her nails into his arms to hold him still, but in less than a minute the strangeness was replaced by heat, and with that heat, passion burst into flame. It smoldered and sizzled between them, fed by Greg's long, fluid strokes. Diandra met the movement of his hips, picking up his rhythm until they were syncopated in the drive toward release.

That release came with a sudden flash of fire. It took Diandra, spun her around until she was dizzy with pleasure, then catapulted her into a moment's break with consciousness. She was barely aware of Greg's hoarse cry, of his stiffening, of the waves of pleasure that rolled over and through him, but deep inside, she felt the warmth of his release, and that brought her a second round of satisfaction.

For a time, the only sounds in the room were of ragged gasps for air. Coming down at length from what he was sure had been the high of his life, Greg rolled to her side, gathered her in his arms and held her close.

He knew the instant she realized what she'd done.

"Don't say it," he whispered, holding her tighter to counter the twinge of tension that winged through her. He raised his voice a bit, but it was hoarse. "Don't say it, because there's no point. What just happened happened because we wanted it. Sure, we could blame it on wine, or on sleep, or on that necklace you're wearing. But the fact is that we're both adults. We're both rational, thinking animals, and we wanted to make love. Period."

She didn't say anything at first, but he felt a subtle relaxation. Bringing one hand to her cheek, he lightly caressed it with his thumb.

"Thank you," she whispered at last.

The movement of his thumb stopped. "For what?"

"For not yelling at me...accusing me of...calling me..." She couldn't quite finish any one of the thoughts, though they were all very much the same. Her first thought when she'd regained her senses was that Greg would think her like her mother. After the beauty of what they'd just shared, the comparison would have hurt badly.

Greg could have returned the thanks, but he wasn't any more eager to think about, much less mention, their parents than she was. So he shifted her in his arms, keeping her very close, and sighed into her hair.

They lay that way for a time, though neither of them spoke. Greg was thinking that he couldn't remember ever being as satisfied—and how remarkable that was. As a lover, Diandra had been a surprise. He'd imagined her to be consummately skilled, but she wasn't. She was eager, but innocent. As hot as she was, she'd let him lead. She'd followed gladly and her touch had been wildly arousing, but not tutored. She'd been very tight. She hadn't made love in a while, and that gave him something to consider.

It gave Diandra something to consider, too, but her thoughts ran along slightly different lines. "Greg?" she whispered.

"Mmm?"

"You're not sterile, are you?"

He was about to burst out with a macho *Are you kidding?* when the oddness of the question hit him. Cautiously he said, "Not that I know of," then asked, "Why?"

"Because . . . I think . . ."

Concerned by the concern in her voice, he held her back and looked down into her face. Even then he was stymied; the room was too dark for him to see much. "What's wrong?"

"We could have a problem," she murmured softly, quickly, apologetically. "I didn't use anything. I don't use anything."

As her meaning hit, Greg sucked in a breath—not so much because he was worried, but because he wasn't. Incredibly a new surge of desire hit him. "Is it a risky time?"

"So-so," she said, trying to sound nonchalant, but her nervousness came through nonetheless.

"Do you get pregnant easily?"

"I don't know," she said, this time in a small wail.

Immediately he gathered her to him. "It's okay. Getting pregnant wouldn't be the end of the world."

"Fine for you to say. You're not the one who'd be affected."

"How do you figure that?"

"Come on, Greg—"

"No, I'm serious. Do you think I'd throw you to the wolves?"

"The wolves being our families, who would go positively nuts after...after..."

Greg pressed her face to his shoulder, muzzling her mouth with his skin. "Don't say it. Please. Not tonight. Tonight's ours, and if a baby comes from it, that's ours, too." His voice lowered. "We'd have a beautiful baby, Diandra."

She moaned against his skin.

"We would," he repeated, mistaking her moan for protest.

"I know," she whispered, not intending protest at all. She was finding the thought of carrying Greg's baby to be shockingly arousing. She was also realizing that she wasn't alone. Greg was obviously affected, too. She wanted to touch him. Lacking the courage to be so bold, she slid her hand to his chest, moved it lightly downward until it came to rest near his navel.

He went very still. "Di?"

She didn't answer, but her lips opened on his collarbone.

"What are you doing?" he asked.

"I don't know. Tell me to stop. This is crazy."

He didn't tell her to stop. Instead, he brought her up with him as he'd done before, only this time he removed her shirt and bra, then took off his own shirt. "I want to know everything this time," he whispered, and before she could remind him that they were increasing the risk each time they made love, he set about doing exactly that.

If the first time had been a hot sweep of passion, this second time was filled with details. Diandra was aware of everything—of the feel of his blunt-tipped fingers on her nipples, the slide of his palms in the hollows of her hips, the slow brush of his thumb over the aching bud between her legs. She was aware of his body, too, of the way she could bring his nipples to pebble hardness, the way his flanks tightened with his arousal, the way he sucked in his stomach when she slid her hand downward.

His fingers entered her first, opening her gently, testing her readiness, and when he looped her legs over his and brought her down on his full erection, he took her cry of delight into his mouth.

When sometime later he carried her to bed, her final thoughts before she drifted to sleep weren't of her parents or the possibility of pregnancy or of the emerald necklace that had pulsed with her climax but of the fact that Greg had claimed her. Greg had made love to her. He'd been the one inside her. That knowledge, more than anything else, filled her to overflowing.

8

Diandra awoke the next morning feeling strangely shy. Being in bed and naked with Gregory York was at the same time very familiar and totally new. Although she'd known him all her life, she'd never known him this way, and the reality of that awareness hit her with the light of day.

Either he was incredibly understanding of her feelings or he was feeling them himself, because he couldn't have handled her better. Kissing her gently, he drew her up and into the shower, then proceeded with normal things—getting dressed, making the bed, fixing breakfast—as if nothing out of the ordinary had happened the night before. She might have been offended had it not been for the fact that whenever she was near he touched her—a hand on her arm or her back, a light kiss on her cheek, an arm around her when he wanted to guide her this way or that. Once or twice, when she looked up in surprise at the touch, she caught a challenging look on his face, but she never raised the protest he dared her to. Without analyzing it, she enjoyed his closeness.

There was passion, but it came in sparks that were tempered by the new gentleness that existed between them. They were at peace with each other, satisfied with the situation as it was for those few moments, hours, perhaps days out of time—which was fortunate, because once breakfast was done and they'd dallied long enough over the morning paper, they had to face the task they'd been sent to do.

That they approached halfheartedly. They forced themselves to catalog the contents of the formal dining room, but when it was time to move on to the family room, which held many of the warm feelings the den had, Greg balked.

"Playtime," he announced, dragging her up from the floor where she'd been sitting with the pad of legal paper that had grown odious to them both.

She pulled back on her hand when he would have had pulled her through the door. "We have to get this done. It's already Thursday."

"I know."

She looked around in despair. "We're barely halfway through."

He pulled her against his shoulder. "I know."

She looked pleadingly up into his face. "I wanted to be back in the office on Monday."

"So did I. But I need a break." He ran his hand up and down her arm. "Come on, Diandra. I can't stand this job. I want to play tennis—and don't say you don't have the clothes for it, because we can get them at the health club. I know you play—at least you used to. You used to come pretty close to beating me."

The natural competitor in Diandra rose to the challenge. "I did, didn't I?"

"But you never quite made it. Want to try again?"

For what seemed an endless moment, she was lost in his eyes. He was her past, but he was much more now, and that much more sent warm currents of pleasure flowing through her. She liked his side pressed to hers, liked his mellow male scent. She wasn't thinking of the fact that they were rivals for the San Francisco store or that their parents had had a tragic affair or that they'd been enemies for years. She was thinking that she felt protected, possessed and possessive. She liked knowing that for these moments out of time Greg was here. If the choice was between sending him off alone to swim or playing tennis with him, there was no choice at all.

Slowly she nodded. When he rewarded her with a kiss, she would have gladly reconsidered the form of activity he'd chosen, but when her eyes said as much, he sent her a chiding stare and led her off.

As with most everything he did in life, Greg played hard. But then so did Diandra. The only problem was that he was physically larger, heavier and stronger than she, hence he had a built-in advantage. Still, she played commendably. While she didn't win a set, she came close, forcing him beyond the six-game-win minimum in two of the three sets they played.

By the time they yielded the court to the next group of players, they were tired and sweaty. Showers in the locker room took care of the sweat; a leisurely lunch at the club's restaurant took care of the tiredness. When they returned to the town house, though, they were no more anxious to tackle the family room than they'd been before.

"Self-discipline is what's needed here," Greg said with a set jaw as he pulled an empty carton to the game cabinet and began to call out the names of the children's games that he packed.

Midway through the second carton, Diandra said, "Wait!" She jumped up from her chair, reached into the box and retrieved the game he'd just set inside. "I *love* Boggle. Let's play."

"I hate Boggle."

"That's because you're not as good at it as you are at tennis. But fair is fair. I played tennis, knowing all along that I'd lose, and I was a good sport about it, wasn't I?"

"It was your own fault you lost. You were too busy looking at my legs to look at the ball."

"That's not true!"

"I saw you, Di. You like the way I look in shorts."

She certainly did, but she wasn't about to admit it. She'd played her hardest on the court. Okay, she'd been distracted once or twice, but mostly during breaks. "I was simply giving back what I got. You did your share of looking, Greg."

"And enjoyed every minute of it," he said with a lascivious grin. Diandra squeezed her eyes shut against its lure, only to open them quickly when he added, "Okay. I'll play Boggle. But on one condition."

Instantly wary, she asked, "What condition?"

He straightened his shoulders. "Whoever loses a round loses an item of clothing."

"*Strip* Boggle? Greg, that's indecent! I mean—" she lowered her voice to a facetious drawl "—poker is one thing. But . . . Boggle?"

"It sure would be fun."

She couldn't argue with that. At the mere suggestion, she'd begun to feel sexy tingles inside. Or maybe it was the way he was standing, so cocksure and manly. Or maybe it was the way he'd been touching her all day. Then again, maybe it had been his legs. They'd been long and lean, just muscular enough, just hairy enough. She'd wanted to touch them, but they'd been too far away.

"What do you say?" Greg asked.

Her eyes flew from his denim-encased thighs to his face, and her cheeks grew pink. A little disgusted with herself for her own lascivious thoughts, she sought to redeem herself. "I'll agree to Strip Boggle under one condition. Whoever loses has to answer a question."

It was Greg's turn to be wary. "What kind of question?"

"Any one the winner wants to ask."

"*Any* question?"

She nodded.

"Like really personal things?"

She shrugged a yes.

Greg wasn't sure he wanted to answer certain personal questions. On the other hand, he had a dozen personal questions he wanted to ask Diandra. He'd agree to her condition in a minute, if he had more faith in his ability to win.

"What's wrong, Greg?" she teased. "Hiding some mighty secrets? Or are you just worried you'll end up naked as a jaybird before I've even taken off my shirt?"

"You're not *that* much better than I am," he said, praying it was true, because he knew he'd play the game. He'd play because he wanted to ask Diandra those questions. The risk of exposing himself was worth it.

"Do we play?" she asked.

"We play."

Pushing the cartons aside, they cleared a space on the carpet, opened the Boggle box and each took a pad of paper and a pen. Diandra shook up the letter cubes, then set them down at the same time that Greg started the timer, and for the next three minutes, they worked in silence. When the timer ran out, Diandra read her list aloud, and they crossed off those words they'd both found. When they scored their remaining words, she was the winner.

Determined to be as good a sport at Boggle as she'd been at tennis, Greg kept his gaze steady. "What'll it be—clothes first, or question?"

Diandra feared that if the clothes went first—particularly in the later stages of the game—she wouldn't be able to concentrate on the question. So she said, "Question," then made some quick calculations. Greg was wearing socks, a shirt, jeans and briefs. Four items. That was it. She had to make the most out of each one.

After a moment, she asked, "Where were you two weeks ago Saturday night at eleven-thirty?"

Greg wasn't sure what he'd expected, but it wasn't that. Brushing his beard with the pad of his thumb, he frowned. "Two weeks ago Saturday night at eleven-thirty? Am I really supposed to remember?"

"Yes."

He closed his eyes and concentrated.

"If you don't answer the question," she told him, "you forfeit another game, which means that you have to take off something else."

His eyes came open. "You're changing the rules."

"No, just making them more specific. Answer the question."

Without pause, he said, "Two weeks ago Saturday night at eleven-thirty, I was in bed."

"With whom?"

"That's another question," he pointed out, but gently. She was curious; that was good. It would also be good for her to hear his answer. "I was alone."

That wasn't what she'd been told. "Really?"

"Really."

"Why?"

"What do you mean, why?" he chided. "I was alone because I chose to be alone. I'd had a busy week, I'd had to go to a cocktail party on Long Island that night, and I was exhausted."

"Did you have a date for the party?"

"I'd gone with Caroline Mann," which was just what Diandra had heard, "but it wasn't a date. We're good friends, that's all. Her lover was off visiting his family in Paris, and she didn't want to drive out alone. I benefited from the arrangement as much as she did. People thought we were together. That spared me some grief.''

"You mean, from other women?"

"Life isn't always easy for a bachelor."

She was pleased enough by what he'd said about Caroline to tease, "Poor thing."

"I'm serious. There are some desperate women out there. They can be pests. I wasn't up for it that night." He put the cover on the cube tray and shook the letter cubes.

"Hold it," she cried. "You have to take something off."

Greg had legitimately forgotten. With a crooked smile doing naughty things to his mouth, he unstrapped his watch.

"Watches don't count," she protested.

"Sure they do. At least," he added in a sensual tone, "they always did in strip poker. And besides," he added as he set the watch on the carpet, "this way you'll have an extra question to ask."

The question Diandra wanted to ask just then was how often and with whom he played strip poker. But thoughts of his stripping made her insides hum, and she had to concentrate. He was shaking up the cubes again.

The letters fell into place. He removed the lid. She set the timer going, and they went to work. When Diandra won that round, too, Greg waited expectantly for her question.

"What went on between you and Jenny Mac-Clain?"

He frowned. "Jenny MacClain is my secretary."

"Your personal secretary. I heard you had an affair with her."

"Who did you hear that from?"

"It doesn't matter. Is it true?"

Greg thought he'd been on top of the gossip. Apparently he'd missed something. "No, it's not true."

"She's a beautiful young woman."

"And a great secretary. She also happens to be married." His gaze grew sharper. "Despite what you may have heard or chosen to believe, I've never had an affair with a married woman. Even aside from the issue of morality, I'm fastidious when it comes to bedmates. The idea of sharing turns me off."

Diandra could almost see the curl of his lips before it blended with his mustache, and it was in keeping with the distaste in his eyes. Mixed in with that distaste was a warning. She waited for him to say something about what he expected of *her* as a bedmate, but as quickly as it had come, the sharpness faded.

"In Jenny's case," he said gently, "there's more. She has a six-year-old child who is severely handicapped. She has to work because she and her husband need the money to pay for special care for the child."

Diandra felt instantly contrite. "I didn't know," she whispered.

"Most people don't, and that's the way Jenny wants it. She's a proud woman. She isn't looking for pity."

"But the gossip—"

"I don't think it occurred to her any more than it occurred to me."

"But she's young and pretty. Didn't you ever wonder what she'd be like—"

"In bed? No. Contrary to popular belief, I don't look at every woman I meet as a potential lover. I've never looked at Jenny that way, and I never will." Having said it all, he tugged off a sock and tossed it aside.

Diandra looked at his foot, then at the one still covered. When she saw that he wasn't moving, she raised her eyes to his. "Each sock separately?"

He nodded. "Gives you one more question. Remember that."

She did, and she assumed that was what distracted her, because she lost the next round.

Greg celebrated his victory with a cocky grin, which faded when he asked, "Who is McKinsey Post?"

She didn't flinch, but said softly, "You know who he is. He's the curator of the museum. I worked with him on a fund-raising effort in January."

"But who is he to you?"

"Someone very nice. Very sensitive. He's a friend."

"He's not married."

"No."

"Gay?"

"Not that I know of."

"Have you slept with him?"

She shook her head.

"Why not?"

"Because I don't want to."

"Why not?"

"Because he doesn't turn me on."

"Like I do?"

Her cheeks went pink as she stared at him. Then, with a shy smile tugging at the corners of her mouth, she said softly, "I suppose there's no point in denying it, is there?"

He shook his head. His eyes skimmed each of her features, slid down her neck, came to rest on the wink of green that showed through the collar of her shirt. He conjured an image of Diandra wearing nothing but that necklace, and his body was fast to respond.

He cleared his throat. "It's mutual." His eyes rose to hers. "Take something off."

Slightly shaky from his perusal, she pressed her lips together and swallowed. Greg had started with his watch, but she'd left hers in the bathroom upstairs. He'd gone on to take off a sock, but she wasn't wearing one, let alone two. Her hand went to the necklace, but she didn't want to—couldn't—take it off.

"This isn't fair," she complained. "You're wearing more than I am."

He shrugged smugly. "You knew that from the start."

Actually she hadn't. She'd counted how many things *he* had on to remove, but she hadn't thought about herself. Moreover, she hadn't counted on losing a game.

Again she pressed her lips together, this time moistening them first. She didn't have many options.

Without raising a fuss, she shifted to her knees, un-snapped and unzipped her jeans, shifted back to her bottom and slid them off. Her shirttails covered her panties, but her legs were bare. She tucked them beneath her.

"Cold?" Greg asked in a voice that was anything but.

She shook her head and reached for the Boggle tray. When the cubes had been sufficiently jumbled, she put them down. Greg set the timer, and they were off.

There had been times during family vacations when Diandra had played Boggle for hours on end, hence she was far from a novice. She knew the kinds of words to look for and the directions. She could easily recognize a tough arrangement of cubes when it came.

This one wasn't. It had a comfortable assortment of consonants and vowels and should have yielded a healthy number of four- and five-letter words, as well as three-letter ones. Her hand seemed to be steadily working, writing down words, but when time ran out, her list wasn't as long as she'd expected.

Greg's was that much shorter.

Relieved, she put down her pen and asked quietly, "Are you seeing anyone special now?"

Beyond curious, she seemed unsure, almost as though she hadn't wanted to ask the question but needed to know the answer. That made Greg feel better. "No. No one special."

"Why not?"

"Special women are hard to come by."

"Who was the last one you had?"

"Had—as in sex, or relationship?"

Diandra hesitated for just a minute before saying, "Both."

"Corinne."

"It's been a while since Corinne," Diandra said, surprised that there hadn't been anyone more recently. "I liked Corinne."

"Me too."

"So what happened?"

"She began to crowd me."

It was a poor choice of words. Diandra reacted with quick sarcasm. "She threatened your freedom. She should have known better."

"It wasn't like that—not the way you make it sound. She began to press for marriage and a family, and I wasn't ready."

"Wasn't ready?"

"Didn't want it. Not with her. We weren't right that way."

"But you two were okay in bed."

Frustrated, he shot a glance out the window. "Why do you have to reduce everything to its lowest common denominator?" He looked back at her in a punishing sort of way. "Yes, we were okay in bed—better than okay—really good. And we got along well for the few nights a week that we were together. But I couldn't think of growing old with her, and that's what marriage means."

Diandra was left without a quick rejoinder. She was surprised that Greg thought about things like growing old. She was even more surprised that he thought about growing old with a woman. She'd have assumed he wouldn't mind little dalliances here and there. He'd been free for so many years that she'd have guessed he'd have trouble settling down.

She was still trying to think of something to say when, with a cavalier flourish, Greg peeled off his other sock, tossed it aside and eyed her expectantly.

"One sock at a time," she grumbled, shifting her bare legs, "is really cheap."

He grinned, shrugged, then reached for the tray of letter cubes.

Diandra won again. "Tell me about your bedroom," she said.

Greg had been wondering which bit of gossip she'd focus on next. He hadn't considered that she'd be curious about his bedroom. "It's a bedroom. What can I say?"

"Is it nice?"

"I suppose. It was professionally decorated, like yours. I haven't paid much attention to the details."

"Because you're otherwise occupied when you get there?"

"No," he said with careful enunciation, "because I'm usually exhausted when I get there, and when I wake up in the morning, I'm in a rush leave."

"When do you go to bed?"

"After the news."

"On nights you're home. How about on nights you're out?"

"I'm not out that often."

"How often?"

"Once or twice a week. Mostly business things. How about you?"

"The same. Is your bedroom big?"

"Big enough to hold a bed, a couple of dressers and a chair."

"King-size bed?"

He nodded.

"What's the color scheme?"

"Navy and gray. It's just a room. Call it attractive or modern or chic or anything else, but it's just a room. A little cold, if you ask me."

Diandra wanted to ask whether he'd ever thought to warm it up, but just then she wanted to be warmed herself, and that would happen as soon as she stopped talking.

So she stopped talking. Looking directly into Greg's eyes, she waited.

One by one, he released the buttons of his shirt. He shrugged out of it. It fell to the rug.

She dropped her eyes to his chest. It was broad at the top and liberally sprinkled with tawny brown hair. Above it, his shoulders were straight and strong, skin stretched tightly over muscle that was firm and naturally earned. Below it, both body and hair tapered toward a slim waist and hips. His stomach rippled faintly thanks to the way he was sitting with one knee bent and the other leg folded beneath. That faint rippling provided an appealing softness. Every bit as appealing was the hint of a navel, cut off by the band of his jeans.

By the time she raised her eyes to his again, her breath was coming slightly faster.

"Okay?" he asked in a husky tone.

She nodded. Too late she realized that she wasn't. She lost the next round.

"Who was your first lover?" Greg asked. He'd been wondering about that. It occurred to him that he'd been wondering about it for years.

"You don't really want to know," Diandra murmured a bit uncomfortably.

"I do."

She hesitated. "It's really not important."

"But it's my question."

"It's not relevant to anything."

"None of this is. But I won the round. Answer the question."

She looked at him for a minute, then looked away and said, "Tommy Nolan."

"Pardon me?"

Looking back, she said more clearly, "Tommy Nolan."

Greg was surprised. He was also a little hurt, though he had no right to be. Tommy Nolan had been one of his best friends for a time. They'd gone to prep school together, and though they'd parted ways when they'd gone off to college, they'd still seen each other from time to time. Apparently, during one of those times, Tommy had seen Diandra, too.

"Tommy Nolan," he repeated softly, a bit dryly. "Good old Tommy."

Feeling awkward, Diandra shrugged.

"How old were you?" he asked.

"Twenty-three."

Greg's eyes widened. "That old? You mean, you went through college a virgin?"

Her chin rose. "Something wrong with that?"

"No, no. I'm surprised, that's all." He'd fully expected that she'd been deflowered at seventeen. Twenty-three was remarkable. "Why Tommy?"

"I really liked Tommy."

"So did I, but I didn't go to bed with him."

"I'm relieved to hear that."

"I can't believe you did."

"Why not?"

He shrugged. "Tommy was my friend."

"Should I have disliked him because I disliked you?"

"No, maybe it was the reverse. Maybe you went with him to spite me."

Diandra snorted. "That's ridiculous. You two weren't all that close at the time. There was no reason you'd have known what happened between him and me, so if I'd wanted to spite you, it wouldn't have worked."

Greg regarded her sadly. "Tommy Nolan. I'd never have guessed."

It was the sadness that got to her. "You're making too much of this, Greg," she told him. "I felt comfortable with Tommy. He was like family in some ways. He was tall and handsome, ambitious, interesting. He reminded me a lot of you."

"Was that why you did it?" Greg asked on impulse.

She was struck speechless as the question echoed in her mind. The thought that she'd been attracted to Tommy specifically because he reminded her of Greg had never occurred to her. It didn't make sense; she'd disliked Greg so.

Then again, it would never have occurred to her that she'd be with Greg now, and when she tried to think of all those things she disliked about him, she felt confused. Too many things were happening too fast. She needed time to think.

Bowing her head, she pressed two fingers to her temple and closed her eyes.

"Diandra?"

She looked up.

His gaze fell with deliberate intent to her shirt.

The game. She remembered the game, and a wave of awareness swept through her. With hands that trembled slightly, she unbuttoned her shirt and let it slip from her shoulders.

Greg was the one to tremble then. Diandra was beautiful, so beautiful. Sitting opposite him with her legs tucked beneath her, wearing nothing but lace panties, a matching bra and the emerald necklace, she was a sight to behold. Her skin was smooth and cream colored, her limbs graceful. The slenderness of her torso was relieved by the most feminine of curves. She couldn't have looked more sexy if she'd been stark naked.

He cleared his throat. "Okay?"

She nodded.

With an effort, he redirected his eyes toward the cube tray. He shook it with more force than was absolutely necessary, then set the timer himself. The arrangement of letters was awkward this time. He managed to compose a few words, then twisted his head to view the letters from a different angle. By the time the timer ran out, he was sure he'd listed a record low number of words. Diandra hadn't done much better, but still she won.

"What do you dream about?" she asked quietly.

"Middle-of-the-night kind of dream?"

"No. Daydream. Wish. Hope for."

In Greg's opinion, it was the most personal question she'd asked yet. She had her sights on his thoughts, and when it came to those, he was vulnerable. But she looked vulnerable, too, sitting there in her bra and panties, awaiting his answer. The emerald necklace glimmered its encouragement, giving him the final impetus to speak.

"I dream about success," he began. "I want to do well within the company."

"I already know that. Tell me something else."

"I want success beyond the company."

A tiny frown ghosted over her brow. "In what way?"

"For nearly fifteen years, the company has been my life. That's not healthy. I want to change it."

"How?"

He hesitated. He could take his clothes off in a minute, bare his body to her eyes. Baring his thoughts was harder. For a split second, he wondered if he had the courage. Then he realized that if he didn't, he was truly a loser in the game.

"I want a family," he said. "I want to be able to come home at night to the woman I love. I want the children we'll have, and I want to be there when they grow up." He paused, pursed his lips contemplatively, looked down. "I dream about lying in a meadow on a warm, sunny day. My woman is in my arms, and we're watching our children play." Without looking up, he shrugged. "I dream about sitting before a warm fire in the cold of winter. Same thing—woman in my arms, kids playing."

He raised his eyes. "I want a home that's a haven from the world, and I want to know that no one and nothing can take that away."

The flow of his words ended as quickly as it had begun, leaving Diandra with a tight knot in her throat. She didn't doubt for a minute that he meant what he said; the heart-rending look in his eyes vouched for it. What she couldn't understand was why she'd never known that he had this side, why she'd never guessed it. She supposed she'd been too busy bickering with him to wonder why he did what he did. She'd been too busy looking for the bad to see the good.

Aware of a slow gathering of tears in her eyes, she averted them. But Greg saw. He felt those tears as shards of pain deep inside. "Diandra?"

She held up a hand, needing that minute to compose herself.

Coming forward on his knees, he reached over and touched her cheek. "What's wrong?"

She shook her head, took a deep breath, then raised her eyes. "I'm okay."

"You felt something."

She nodded and said in a very soft voice, "Your dreams aren't far off from mine. Ironic, isn't it—that we're both in such enviable professional positions, but still we want more? Where does it end, do you think? If we find a haven, will we want something else?"

"I can't imagine anything I'd want beyond that."

"Me either." She took a shaky breath. "There are times, though, when it feels like an impossible dream. Do you think we'll ever get there?"

Greg didn't know the answer to that, and something odd had just struck him. When he'd been describing the dream to Diandra, she'd been the woman in it. She fitted his dream. Looking down at her, he suddenly wanted her on a myriad of different levels.

Unable to fully understand what that meant, he picked the one of those levels that was clearest. Lowering his head, he put a light kiss on her lips, then sat back and reached for the snap of his jeans.

Diandra caught her breath. Holding it, she watched him open the snap and lower the zipper. He stood and pushed the denim to his thighs, then off one foot, then the other. Then he returned to his perch on the rug, but not before she'd learned two things. The first was that he looked wonderful in nothing but hip-hugging white briefs. The second was that he was aroused.

Her eyes flew to his.

"You can't be surprised," he chided.

She nodded, then as quickly shook her head.

"You could always get more of a rise out of me than any other woman I know," he said, which was exactly the kind of suggestive statement that, in the past, would have brought an angry response from Diandra.

She remained quiet, though. It occurred to her that she wanted to get more of a rise from him—both emotionally and physically. The meaning of that left her unsettled, which, she assumed, was why she lost the next round of Boggle.

"Tell me a fantasy," Greg ordered in a throbbingly low voice.

She swallowed. "Fantasy?"

"Sexual fantasy."

"I don't have any."

"Sure you do. Don't be shy. I'll tell you mine if you tell me yours."

"I don't have any."

"Everyone has sexual fantasies."

She shook her head. "Not me."

"Come on, Di. You're like fire in my arms. You're a very passionate woman."

"I've never thought of myself that way." At his dubious look, she said, "I'm not all that experienced. Couldn't you tell?"

Thinking back, he could. Her responses to him had been innocent. She'd followed his lead, gained courage as she'd gone along. Still, she was a very passionate woman. "Surely you've imagined sexy things."

She shook her head. "I figured that if I imagined them, I'd want them, and if I couldn't get them, I'd be frustrated."

She was making a statement about her past, and Greg would have been deaf not to hear. He'd put money on the fact that she could realize any fantasy she wanted in his arms.

"I still think you're shy," he teased, but didn't push the issue because his mind was already zipping ahead. Diandra had lost a round. Another item of clothing had to go. "The bra," he breathed, dropping his gaze to that piece of lace. "Take off the bra."

For a minute, Diandra didn't move. Then her hands met at the front catch of her bra. She twisted it, released it, peeled the lace cups from her breasts and the straps from her shoulders. The air felt cool on her newly exposed skin, but she was so warm inside that she barely noticed.

Greg was the one with goose bumps. He wasn't sure how much more he could take of watching Diandra undress piece by piece. If he'd thought her sexy in her bra and panties, he had to redefine the word to describe what she looked like now. She was sitting demurely, her legs folded gracefully to one side. Her chin had the slightest downward tilt, causing her hair to brush her cheeks, and her bangs had an unintended part. Her shoulders were straight, made positively regal by the emerald necklace that lay pulsing around her neck, and beneath it were her breasts. Firm and nicely rounded, they were alabaster in the soft light of late day that filtered in through the window.

He was aware that while he was feeling shaky most everywhere else, that part between his legs was solid as a rock. If he hadn't been a man of self-control, he'd have lunged at her then and there. But the game wasn't through.

"Still okay?" he whispered, half-wishing she'd shake her head so he could take her in his arms.

She nodded. The game was nearly over. One more round, and one of them would be naked. Dragging her eyes from his, she focused on the letter cubes for the last time.

Neither of them was sharp. But then, neither of them was concentrating on the game. When Diandra managed to score ten points more than Greg, the victory seemed anticlimactic.

"Last chance," he warned softly as he waited for her question.

"*Your* fantasy," she said in a breathy tone. "I want to know yours."

"I have more than one."

Her voice fell to a whisper. "Tell me the most erotic one."

Her whisper seared him. He was already painfully aroused, and she wanted a retelling of his most erotic fantasy. He would have laughed, except that there was nothing funny about the fantasy. Nor was there anything funny about his revealing it to Diandra. He'd never shared his most intimate thoughts with a woman before. That he was about to share them with Diandra was telling.

"I fantasize," he said quietly, "that I've been imprisoned in a room with a woman I don't know. I can't see her, because it's night and the room is pitch-black. Our lives are in danger. We need each other to survive, which means sharing a very basic trust, but the only way we can build that trust is by making love." His view grew lower, more hoarse. "So we do. We make love to each other first in traditional ways, then in more unusual ways, then even more sensual ways, then risqué ways. Still I can't see her, but my hands and mouth know her. My body knows her. She is warm and gentle, a little adventurous, very beautiful in my mind's eye." He paused, then said softly, "I trust her with my life."

"Do you love her?" Diandra heard herself ask.

"It's just a fantasy."

"But do you love her?"

"I trust her. I suppose I'd love her if I had a chance, but the fantasy always ends too soon."

"Sad," Diandra whispered.

But Greg was no longer thinking of the fantasy. He was thinking that his body was aching for Diandra, and that just then he needed her desperately. Too aroused to let pride stand in the way, he eased his briefs over his hardness and tossed them aside. Then, sitting back on his heels with the blood pounding from his heart to his groin and back, he waited for her to make her move.

Diandra couldn't take her eyes from him. She'd never seen a man as glorious, and she knew she never would. He was maleness at its best. He was Gregory

York, and he wanted her, wanted her in a very beautiful way.

With the explosion of wild emotions inside, she came up on her knees and crossed the short distance to where he knelt. She put her fingertips to his mouth, slid them gently inside, drew them out only when her lips covered his. Her damp fingers found their way down his body to that part of him that was swollen with need. They closed on him and gently began to stroke.

"I need you, Greg," she whispered into his mouth. "Make love to me like you made love to her. Trust me that way."

Wanting her more than he'd wanted anything before, Greg slid his hands up her sides. He tried to temper his need by holding her lightly, but the brush of her nipples against his chest was his undoing. When his mouth took hers, there was no holding back. While his passion became hers, trust was the fuel that sent them higher and higher through the night.

9

Given the length and intensity of their lovemaking, Diandra should have slept until noon the next day. But she was awake at dawn, lying silently beside Greg, wondering how she was going to handle the fact that she was in love.

On the one hand, it made such sense. Their families' fates were intricately entwined.

Then again, it made no sense at all. Diandra had spent years detesting first Greg, then his father, too. True, she saw Greg in a different light now. But she didn't think she'd ever forgive his father; that was bound to be a bone of contention between them.

And then there was the issue of work. She and Greg were vice presidents of the same corporation, but they were rivals for the San Francisco store, which was still very much up for grabs.

And all that was before she considered Greg's feelings for her. She loved him, but did he love her? He'd never once said the words, despite all they'd done to each other the night before—and they'd done a lot. Diandra hadn't imagined that two people could do what they'd done. Even now, thinking back on it, she blushed.

But did he love her?

Carefully she turned her head to look at him. He was sprawled on his back, sleeping soundly, his hair mussed, his features relaxed. In the past hours, those features had become nearly as familiar to her as her own, and more dear.

There was a vague sense of unreality to it. They'd been cooped up together for four days, partners in a task neither of them wanted to do. Their normal lives were a world away. They were in a limbo of sorts, and therefore vulnerable when they might not normally have been so.

Her hand went to the emerald necklace. For what had to be the hundredth time since Monday, she wondered at its power. It hadn't made her love Greg; she'd done that on her own. But the necklace had created the force field in which she'd acted. Would the force field disintegrate once the necklace was removed? Would her feelings for Greg fizzle?

She didn't know the answers to those questions, or to the others that chipped away at the peace she'd found in Greg's arms. The future held such promise—yet no promise at all. She felt as though she were once more back in that boxwood labyrinth, lost and confused, not knowing which way to turn.

What she needed, she realized, was to return to familiar ground. She needed not only to think, but to think under circumstances that were normal. She needed to view what had happened from the world she knew in the hope that she could make some sense of it.

That meant leaving. The very thought of it created a void inside her, but it seemed the only way. She couldn't think straight as long as Greg was around, and while there was something beautiful about that, it was also frightening. He held a power over her, always had, always would. She had to know exactly how vulnerable she was.

With a final, heart-wrenching look at him, she crept silently from his bed and returned to her room, where she put on the business clothes she'd worn Monday and packed the few other things she'd brought. Then she stole down the stairs to the living room. Pausing before the marble mantel, she bowed her head and closed her eyes in a silent prayer that she was doing the right thing. Hands trembling, she removed the emerald necklace. She held it to her cheek for a lingering moment before returning it to its box. Then, hurrying lest she change her mind, she let herself out into the early morning air.

"What in the hell did you do that for?" Greg bellowed over the line late that day. "I thought we'd established something last night. How do you think it felt to wake up and find out you'd gone?" He snorted. "So much for trust. And what about respect? You didn't even bother to leave a note. Did you think I wouldn't worry? I assumed you'd go straight to the office, but no, not you. And you didn't go home, either; I've been trying this number for hours. Where in the hell have you *been*?" Before she could answer, he raced on, "I thought we'd straightened a few things out, but I was wrong. You must still think I'm an insensitive clod if you thought I'd let you go without a word. I was *worried*, Diandra." He gave a harsh guffaw. "But I suppose that wouldn't mean anything to you. You're just as selfish as ever. Or maybe it's that you're a coward. You ran out of here because you couldn't face what was happening. Maybe you thought I'd start making demands on your precious time. Is the idea of fidelity that odious to you? Or is it San Francisco that's got you in a snit? Or," he went on in an icy voice, "was it your warped idea of revenge? You'd string me along until I was hooked, then leave me in the lurch? Did it feel good walking out on me like that? Huh? *Answer me*, Diandra."

But she couldn't. Her eyes were filled with tears, and there was a huge lump in her throat that wouldn't allow for any sound at all.

Greg didn't have that problem. "Well, let me tell you something, sweetheart. Two can play the game. You may have given me the best time I've had in bed in months, but you're not the only woman in town. Not by a long shot." The connection was severed with an abrupt click.

Diandra held the phone to her ear for another minute, then let it slowly fall past her cheek and neck to her breast. Ducking her head low, she began to cry. She pressed the phone to the ache in her chest, and when that didn't help she began to sway back and forth. The ache persisted, and the tears kept coming.

There had been more times in her life than she cared to count when Diandra had felt alone. The earliest times had been when she'd wanted her mother, but her mother hadn't been around. There had been times during college when she'd wanted nothing more than to be tied to a man who was tied to her, but the right man had never come along. So she'd graduated, earned an advanced degree and immersed herself in CayCorp. Even then, after long days at the office, she'd too often come home feeling as empty as her apartment.

But she'd never felt more alone than she did just then.

How long she stood holding the dead receiver in her hand she didn't know. Gradually she stopped crying, and still she stood, not knowing where to go or what to do. At length, when she realized that she was cold, she replaced the receiver, went into the bedroom and climbed under the covers. There, huddled beneath satin sheets and a handmade comforter, she cried herself to sleep.

First thing Saturday morning, after deciding that life must go on, Diandra went to work. Her office was as it had been when she'd left it the Monday before, except for the pile of papers on the desk. Distractedly she flipped through them, pulled out several for closer study, then set them aside and spent the next hour looking out the window. She was grateful that her secretary wasn't there to witness her idleness; she'd have thought her sick.

Heartsick was the correct term, though Diandra tried not to dwell on it. When she couldn't muster interest in the papers on her desk, she went shopping— not at Casey and York, but in the small boutiques of Georgetown.

The Saturday crowds were moderate, comforting in ways, since they assured her anonymity, disturbing in others, since they were largely made up of people in pairs or larger groups that, by comparison, made her feel all the more single. Still, she weathered them as the lesser of the evils. She didn't relish the idea of returning to her apartment alone.

Three times she passed public phones. Three times she bit her lip and silently debated making calls.

The first time, she thought of the party that was being given by a friend in Virginia. She'd been invited but had refused the invitation well before she'd gone to Boston, simply because she was tired of parties. Her feelings hadn't changed.

The second time, she thought of Anthony Adams. He was nothing more than a friend, and she needed a friend. But he'd ask questions she wouldn't want to answer. And besides, friend or not, she felt disloyal running to Anthony.

The third time, she thought of Greg. That time she turned away, knowing that her call wouldn't be welcome. He wasn't thinking highly of her. She'd only be asking for grief.

Time and again as she walked her hand went to her throat. Once the saleswoman in a lingerie boutique even eyed her in alarm, as though expecting her to keel over choking, and Diandra assumed she'd been looking as pained as she felt. It was absurd, she knew, but she felt raw. The emerald necklace had become part of her. Its removal had left an open wound.

In the end, for sheer lack of energy, she did go home, where she spent an unheard-of night in front of the television. She fell asleep there; she awoke there. Angry at herself, at Greg, at the world, she took jeans from the bag she'd never unpacked, threw on a sweater and sneakers and went out to walk through Washington like a tourist.

She was so lonely. It amazed her, because she'd only been with Greg for four days, but she kept remembering the things they'd done together, and her loneliness increased. Her only hope was that when she got back to work on Monday, when her office was full of the people who seemed to stream in and out on a regular basis, she'd feel more like herself. At least then she'd be able to deal with the loneliness. She always had in the past. She supposed she could do it again.

When she got back to work on Monday, her office was indeed full of the people who seemed to stream in and out on a regular basis, but they offered no relief from her pain. Though she dealt with each in a competent manner, competence was all they got. Her heart was elsewhere.

By the end of the day, she was beginning to wonder whether things would ever be the same again. The world seemed monochromatic. She couldn't garner enthusiasm for much at all.

It was almost a relief when an irate Bart called to demand her presence in Palm Beach the next morning. He gave no details, barely allowed her a word. He made it clear that she was to be there with no questions asked.

She went. She flew down by commercial airline, thinking that though she'd made the same trip a mere ten days before, it seemed more like a year. With that earlier trip on her mind, she half-expected to find Greg in Bart's penthouse. When she didn't, she felt simultaneously relieved and disappointed.

Both of those sentiments were premature. She'd simply arrived before him. Half an hour later and only minutes after a scowling Bart joined her on the patio, Greg came through the door looking like thunder.

"This had better be good, Bart," he growled, too consumed by his own anger to note Bart's. "You're pushing it."

Bart's voice rang as loudly as his age and style would allow. "I'll push it as far as I want, mister. I want some answers, and I want them now." His eyes flashed from Greg to Diandra and back. "What happened?"

Diandra was suffering too much to answer. Seeing Greg was bad enough; feeling the force of his angry gaze was like having a knife twisting in the wound.

"What happened," Greg seethed, "is that you sent us to do your dirty work. You didn't want to wade through all that stuff—"

"Not the town house," Bart interrupted with the sharp wave of a gnarled hand. "I don't give a hoot about that. What happened to the necklace?"

Greg shifted his glare to Greg before returning it to Bart. "Nothing happened to the necklace. We left it on the mantel right where we found it."

"But it was supposed to work!" Bart claimed indignantly. "It was supposed to work like a charm!" He looked at Diandra. "Yet you ran out of there early Friday morning—" his eyes flew to Greg "—and you left that afternoon, and neither of you spoke to the other all weekend, and you were zombies in the office yesterday.''

Diandra was beginning to come around. Something was strange about what Bart was saying, strange enough to temporarily blunt her pain. "What are you talking about?" she asked cautiously.

"The *necklace!*" he shouted, then began to cough.

She shot a worried look at Greg. Sliding from her chair to the next, she put a hand on Bart's. "Relax. Please. Whatever it is isn't worth choking over."

Bart took one breath, coughed again, took another breath, then a third. He seemed to be calming himself by sheer force of will, and indeed, when he spoke again, his voice was more even. "That necklace is part of a set they call the Montclair Emeralds."

Diandra looked questioningly at Greg, who looked questioningly back.

Bart explained. "Charles de Montclair was a renegade Frenchman. As the legend goes, he lost his heart to a beautiful woman, stole her from the powerful duke to whom she'd been betrothed and brought her to live with him on his secluded estate. As a token of his undying love, he presented her with the emeralds. They were passed from generation to generation until the time of the French Revolution, when the couple's great-great-granddaughter fled to America. There, for the sake of survival, she was forced to sell the jewels one by one."

His tale ended. The echo of waves rolling onto the shore filled the background, but Diandra didn't hear. Her heart was thudding too loudly.

"How did you get the necklace?" she asked.

"I bought it from a friend, a collector. He said it was like Cupid's arrow. He assured me it would work."

She swallowed. "Work how? What was it supposed to do?"

Bart's furrowed brow grew all the more so. "Bring you two together!" He was clearly annoyed that they'd missed the point. "You're perfect for each other! Even a blind man could see it. You're a match physically and intellectually. You share a professional interest. You've never married, either of you, because there's no one else who can give you a run for your money. You're the best these families has come up with in years. You belong together. But you're so *damned bullheaded* that you can't see it for yourselves."

"So you decided to give us a push," Diandra murmured in dismay.

Greg was appalled. "You sent us up there on that cock-and-bull mission just to throw us in with that necklace?"

"It wasn't a cock-and-bull mission," Bart argued. "The town house had to be closed up sometime."

"But you don't have a buyer, do you?" Diandra asked. She was feeling the beginnings of the same slow burn that she'd heard in Greg's voice.

"I have buyers all the time. I just turn them down."

"But you told us you had one and that you needed the town house closed quickly. You used us, Bart. How could you have done that?"

"I did what I thought was right."

"Well, it wasn't," Greg told him. "Diandra and I are adults. We have a right to know what we're doing and why, and we have a right to decide for ourselves who to love."

"You can't force something like that on people," Diandra added, but Bart had a ready answer.

"I didn't force a thing. The necklace was supposed to do it without your even knowing."

"The necklace," Greg muttered. "Without us even knowing—fat chance! That necklace may be a magnificent piece of jewelry, but subtle it isn't. We felt its force from the start."

Bart old face brightened. "You did? That's a good sign. Maybe you just left too early. You didn't give it long enough to work."

"Oh, Bart, you aren't *listening*," Diandra cried. "That necklace—*no* necklace—is magical. It can't perform miracles. It can't do something that isn't supposed to be."

"But you *are* supposed to be," Bart insisted. His hopeful expression made him look every bit the leprechaun. "You and Greg should have been together years ago."

Greg shook his head with force. "Impossible."

Diandra agreed. "Greg and I have rubbed each other the wrong way since we were kids, and that was even before the business with..." She didn't want to say it.

Bart did, and with surprising composure. "With your parents? That business with your parents happened at a vulnerable time for both of you. If it hadn't been for that, I'm *sure* you'd have been together. It was destined that one day a Casey and a York would fall in love." He glanced off toward the sea, looking sober, and said in a sad voice, "It happened once, but too late. If only the timing had been better."

Greg was furious. "That whole *thing* sucked. There wasn't any love involved."

Diandra agreed. "It was pure lust."

"She seduced him—"

"He seduced her—"

"Keep still, both of you," Bart growled. "This is hard enough for me without your degenerating into juveniles spatting." Then he admitted on a note of defeat what he'd been too proud, after the stance he'd originally taken, to confess to any other family members. "There was no seducing done. They fell in love." He raised a hand as though to say, That's all, then dropped it back to his lap.

For a minute neither Greg nor Diandra spoke. They were too surprised to utter a word.

Greg was the first to recover. His tone was harsh and skeptical. "She didn't seduce him?"

Bart shook his head.

Diandra was as disbelieving as Greg. "Love?"

Bart nodded.

Greg waited for an explanation. When it didn't come, he burst out with, "Do you know what you're saying? You're saying that your son willingly betrayed both his wife and his best friend to have an affair with Abby. Willingly, Bart. That's some indictment. And it's a far different story from the one you've always told."

"I was hurt. Angry, at first. Disillusioned."

Straightening in her seat, Diandra took her own shot. "You blamed my mother for what happened. You looked at her like she was something dirty, something cheap. Every time her name came up, you turned your back."

"I was wrong," he said quietly. Slowly he added, "I didn't know then what I know now."

For the second time in as many minutes, a silence hung over his words. It was a very cautious Diandra who broke it this time.

"Do you know something that we don't?"

Looking uncomfortable, he said, "I found letters, letters from Abby to Greg. They were in my den. Greg must have stashed them there at some point. Maybe he wanted them found—I don't know—but I came across them by accident and I read every one."

Diandra was sitting on the edge of her seat, her hands tightly clasped in her lap. "What did they say?"

Bart sniffed in a breath in prelude to a reluctant confession. "She loved him. She was torn apart by that love. She felt guilty, because she knew that John and Sophia were being hurt. She kept asking what to do."

"And we'll never know what he said, will we?" Greg snapped. He was standing with his back rigid and his features tense, looking as dark as Diandra had ever seen him look.

"Not in his own hand," Bart conceded. In the wake of Greg's resistance, his confession became more forceful. "But some of it came through in Abby's letters. She wrote things like, 'You told me you feel the guilt,' or 'You love us both, Sophia and me,' or 'I'm glad last weekend meant as much to you as it did to me.' It was clear that they shared something special. It was also clear from the letters that they tried to control themselves.''

Greg snorted.

Bart stared him down, gaining even greater strength as he spoke on. ''At one point in her letters, Abby talked about years. That may have been how long their feelings for each other were simmering, and if so they have to be admired for fighting it as long as they did. It's possible that much of Abby's flitting was an attempt to escape her feelings for Greg. They were lovers who met at the wrong time, but what they felt was so strong that they couldn't stop it.''

''Lust,'' Greg muttered. ''Maybe mutual, but pure lust.''

But Bart was shaking his head. ''*No*. It was more than that. Apparently I knew my son better than you knew your father. He was a man who loved—he loved your mother, he loved you, and in the final years of his life he loved Abby. His mistake—*their* mistake, perhaps—was that they never made a choice. Abby couldn't cut off what she felt for John and Diandra anymore than Greg could cut off what he felt for your mother and you.''

Switching his gaze to Diandra, he held up a hand. ''I'm not saying that Abby was the best of mothers to begin with, any more than Greg was the best of fathers. They were who they were, but they tried. They tried to do it all and did none of it justice. In the end, they were probably as unhappy, if not more so, than the rest of us.''

Greg swore softly. "Are you suggesting that they committed suicide in that plane?"

"No," Bart said gruffly. "I don't believe that. I can't believe it. And in any case, we'll never know. But the point is that if what happened between your parents is what's keeping you and Diandra apart, it shouldn't. You belong together. Abby and Greg came so close; you two could clinch it. It would be a damn shame if the love your parents shared is the one thing that prevents you from sharing your own." He paused for an instant, then went on with an air of belligerence. "These families were meant to be united. I want a Casey to marry a York, and I want to see it before I die."

"Dammit," Greg barked, "you can't program love! You can't just order it up!"

But that wasn't what Bart wanted to hear. Scowling at the patio tiles, suddenly looking and sounding every bit his eighty-four-years of age, he muttered, "The necklace was supposed to do it. Miller promised me it would work. I paid a pretty penny, and what do I have to show for it? Two disgruntled children and a messy town house."

"The town house," Diandra echoed in a high voice. "I don't believe you're worried about the town house."

"Frederick can get a crew to pack up in a day," Greg said angrily, "and as for two disgruntled children, we wouldn't be disgruntled at all if you hadn't butted in. Dammit, Bart," he went on in an ominous voice, "I don't like being manipulated. It's an insult to my intelligence."

Undaunted, Bart said, "So I maneuvered you up to Boston. I needed the work done, and you're family. I had a right to ask."

Diandra was feeling as angry as Greg. "You didn't ask. You ordered. Even when we suggested alternatives, you insisted that we do it your way. But the *worst* of it was that you held us hostage. You dangled something in front of us that you knew we both wanted."

Bart stared at her hard. "I never once tied San Francisco to that job."

"Maybe not verbally," Greg argued, "but it was right there, the perfect lure. You knew we both wanted it, and you knew that neither of us would give the other the edge by begging off the Boston job. Well, let me tell you something—" he began, only to be interrupted by Diandra.

"I don't *want* San Francisco," she declared in as sure a voice as she'd ever used. "You can do what you want with it, but—"

"The appeal is gone. That goes for me, too," Greg said with force. "I've got New York. I'll stay on there."

For the first time, Bart seemed rattled. "But—but you wanted San Francisco from the start."

"I wanted it from *before* the start, but that doesn't matter. If there's one thing I've learned from this mess it's that a store is a store. That's all. Believe it or not, there is more to life than Casey and York." He paused for a split second with a look of utter distaste on his face, then said in a voice that vibrated with anger, "I think you know what you can do with your San Francisco store." Turning on his heel, he stalked from the room.

Diandra would have applauded had she not been as livid. In the minute she took to compose herself, Bart spoke.

"He's angry. When he calms down, he'll realize that he didn't mean what he said."

"He meant it," she said with conviction. "And he's right. A store is a store. Not much of a basis for extortion."

Bart bristled. "Just a minute, young lady. I have never in my life stooped to extortion."

"There are subtle forms of it. But subtle or not, in this case it won't work. I don't want San Francisco."

"Then you're a fool. It's yours for the asking, now that Greg's turned away."

"A fool I may be, but I don't want it. Funny," she said without a hint of a smile, "I can't even remember why I wanted it to begin with." Standing, she slipped the slim strap of her purse over her shoulder.

Bart's frail body stiffened. "You can't leave me in the lurch this way."

"No one's left in the lurch. I can think of a dozen people who want San Francisco and who'd do a great job. You'll have your store."

"But I want that marriage!" he cried.

With the height of emotion passed, the anger that had kept Diandra going began to slip. Beneath it was a soul-deep sadness. "We can't always have what we want," she said. "I'm sorry." She started for the door.

His voice followed her, pleading now. "Try it again, Diandra. That necklace has power, I know it does."

She knew it, too. But the power of a gem was only as good as the strength of its wearer. And at that moment she wasn't feeling strong at all. Fearful that she'd break down in tears, she sent Bart a final tremulous look and quickly left.

Greg flew directly back to New York, but by the time he arrived his anger had gone. In its place was a sense of loss that was more pervasive than he'd have imagined possible.

Acting out of the force of sheer habit, he distractedly climbed into a cab and gave his address. Then he slumped low on the torn leather seat and grappled with that loss.

It had nothing to do with San Francisco. He wasn't at all sorry about his decision. He knew New York. The New York branch of Casey and York was the largest, the most prestigious, the most challenging. Heading the San Francisco branch would be a novelty, but novelties wore off, and then where would he be? He'd be on the West Coast trying to deal with the same problems he'd had to deal with on the East Coast. So what was it worth?

Diandra. It all came back to Diandra. During the four days they'd spent together in Boston, she'd come to mean the world to him. He didn't know how it had happened, certainly didn't believe that the Montclair jewels had created something where it hadn't existed, but he'd come to see things in a new light.

Like Boggle. A new angle, new words. In Boston, he'd seen Diandra in a different context. Apart from CayCorp. Apart from family. She'd been a different woman from the one he'd expected. Then again, he supposed he'd been a different man. More relaxed. More open. More honest.

Wily old Bart.

Greg didn't have to wonder where he'd gone wrong. It had been the phone call he'd made to Diandra in Washington. He'd been such a fool. He'd been overwhelmed by a dozen strange emotions. Unable to deal with them, he'd lashed out in anger. If there had been any chance for them, he'd killed it then.

She hadn't tried calling him back, hadn't tried calling him since. She'd barely said two words to him at Palm Beach, and she'd looked nearly as miserable as he'd felt.

Which was interesting.

Would she have looked so miserable if she didn't care for him?

Would she have declared that she didn't want San Francisco even before he'd said *he* didn't want it—if she weren't sincere in her claim?

Would she have been so innocent in her sexual responses if she'd lived the wild life he'd always assumed?

Would she have given him her soul and then some in bed that last night if she hadn't harbored the same deep and abiding feeling he did?

Coming up in his seat, he instructed the cabbie to head back to the airport. He needed some answers, and there was only one person who had them.

His destination was Washington. But first, he wanted another look at that necklace.

10

Diandra stared at the emerald teardrops and vowed not to cry. She'd done enough crying in the past few days to last her a lifetime, and it hadn't accomplished a thing.

What was called for was action. Action and honesty.

Oh, she'd been plenty honest with Bart. She'd meant what she'd said about San Francisco. She didn't want the assignment, wasn't sure why she ever had. But she hadn't been honest about her feelings for Greg, and that was what needed changing.

Standing before the necklace with her fingers curled over the edge of the marble mantel, she enumerated her mistakes.

First, she never should have left Greg that Friday morning—at least, not in the way she had. She should have told him her plans, should have explained that she was overwhelmed by what had happened. She should have woken him up or left a note or called him later that day. But she hadn't. He'd had a right to be angry.

Second, she should have said something when he'd finally called her. True, she would have had to squeeze

the words out between the lump in her throat and his
anger, but she should have done it somehow.

Third, she should have called him afterward. She'd
had Saturday and Sunday. She should have tried to
contact him, tried to tell him how she felt.

Fourth and finally, in Palm Beach, she could have,
should have spoken up. With all that talk about a love
that was destined to be, she'd had more than one op-
portunity to bare her heart. But there'd been Bart and
his scheming, which had angered her, then the reve-
lations about her mother and Greg's father, which had
shocked her. And there'd been Greg. He hadn't said a
thing about love, hadn't said much about her at all.

But would he have been so short with Bart, right
from the start, if he hadn't been deeply disturbed?

Would he have thrown San Francisco in the old
man's face if something momentous hadn't changed
inside him?

Would there have been as much hurt as anger in his
voice when he'd called her if he hadn't felt something?

Would he have raised the issue of fidelity without
good cause?

She swayed, and the emeralds winked. Indeed, the
necklace was a charm. It had power. Without it, she
and Greg would have bickered their way through those
four days. They'd never have stopped long enough to
give each other a chance. But the necklace could only
do so much. It could no more force deeper emotions
than it could control stubborn pride.

Eyes on the gems, she took one deep breath, then
another. She wasn't about to put the necklace on—she

had to stand on her own this time. But she felt calmer. She knew what had to be done, and she was determined to do it.

Then she heard the sound of a lower door closing. Head whipping around, she stared at the living room archway. Frederick had been on his way out when she'd arrived and had said he'd be gone for the evening. It had been her impression that Mrs. Potts had ceased her cleaning sessions, since Bart was supposedly selling the town house—at least, she hadn't shown up the week before. Nor had any of those other who had keys, not that they would be coming this late in the day.

There was another person who had a key. Just as she did. She held her breath, listening to the rapidly rising patter of muted steps on the stair runners.

Then he appeared. His momentum would have taken him straight into the room had he not caught sight of her first. He came to a stunned halt just inside the archway and stared.

Totally immobile but for the thudding of her heart, Diandra stared right back. *Action and honesty.* The words blinked their subliminal message in her mind, but she was unable to move or speak. To do either would have been to expose her heart's feelings, and she'd spent so many years protecting herself from Greg that she supposed it was a conditioned reflex.

Suddenly it struck her, though, that what had worked during her childhood was now simply a childish response. The woman she was demanded better. The man Greg was deserved more.

But before she could act, Greg did. With slow, sure steps that were in contradiction to the vulnerable look on his face, he crossed the floor to stand before her. His eyes searched hers, asking all the questions he'd wondered about, and in the asking were the answers she wanted. When he raised a hand to her cheek, she tipped her head to his palm.

So little action, so much honesty.

With a low moan, Greg wrapped his arms around her and clasped her so tightly to him that for a minute her toes actually left the ground. She might well have floated. She felt suddenly light-headed and light-hearted, relieved of an awesome weight. Her arms were coiled high around his neck, trembling with the strength of her emotions.

His lips moved against her hair, but his whispered words were sporadic and broken. "Ah . . . Di . . . when I thought . . . of never being close to you again. . . ."

Sinking her hands into his hair, she tugged until his head came up. "Were you in agony?" she whispered soberly.

"Yes."

"So was I."

"Why do we do this to each other?"

"Habit, I think."

"We're fools."

She nodded and put a hand on his beard, wanting to touch, to verify that he was there. "I think we've been fools for a long time."

"How long?"

"Years."

"I think that's how long we've been drawn to each other. We fought because of the attraction. It was there even back then, but we couldn't accept it."

She touched her thumb to the corner of his mouth. "That was dumb of us."

"Stubborn."

"Defensive."

"Shortsighted."

"Self-defeating. Bart was wrong," she decided. "The reason neither of us has settled down is because no one else would *have* us."

Greg's arms rose on her back until his fingertips braced her head. "Will you have me?"

She nodded, then arched both brows to return the question.

"What do you think?" he growled and gave her another bone-crushing hug.

Diandra thought she had to be the happiest woman alive. And the luckiest. To have Greg was to have far more than money could ever buy. He was unique. He was magnificent. He was priceless.

Unique, magnificent, priceless. With her cheek pressed snugly to his collar, she opened her eyes to the emerald necklace. It sat in its box on the mantel, smugly, she thought. At the slight movement of Greg's head, she looked up to find that he, too, was studying it. When he looked back at her, his gaze was dark and intense. It fell to her lips.

Lowering his head, he met her in a deep, heart-throbbing, tongue-tangling, open-mouthed kiss. And by the time either of them spoke again, they were ly-ing spoon fashion on the bed in the Oak Room.

They'd made spectacular love. Their bodies were sated, but their minds were coming to life.

"I love you," Greg whispered against the warm curve of her ear.

Diandra hugged his arm, which lay between her breasts and whispered back, "I love you, too." The words echoed in the silence like a beautiful song. For an encore, she turned her head and instigated another kiss. Then she asked, "When did you know?"

"Know, or admit?"

"Either. Both."

"Know—the last night we spent together. I'd never done those things with another woman. They require trust and devotion and a hunger so intense that it rises above the physical. Admit—when I got back to New York today. I realized that I'd used my anger as a shield. When it slipped, the road ahead looked mighty bleak." He rose on an elbow, caught her chin with his fingers and turned up her face. "I won't have to live through that kind of hell, will I?"

"No."

"You'll marry me?"

"Yes."

He kissed her soundly, then passionately, but passion became gentleness when he felt an overpowering need to talk. Settling her back against him again, he said, "You bring out sides of me that no other woman has. I've never felt tender or possessive or protective before, but I feel those things with you." He sighed deeply. "Besides, you're a tough opponent. I like it better when we're on the same side."

"You could always win."

"I want *us* to win."

The fullness of love welled within Diandra. It was several minutes before she spoke again. "I want *us* to win, too. How will we manage it with work?"

"Are you tied to Washington?"

"No, but you've got New York neatly taken care of. There'd be nothing for me to do there."

"That's good, because I'm tired of New York. I was thinking of—"

"Boston, why don't we try Boston?" she asked, squirming onto her back and looking up into his face. "Let Alex take San Francisco. He's done a super job with the store here; he'd be great there. He'd consider it a personal victory if Bart gave it to him. We could convince Bart to do it."

"In a minute. He owes us."

The flicker of a frown crossed her brow. "Or do we owe him?"

"I think it's a little of both, but don't tell him that. He deserves to feel guilty."

"He'll get pleasure out of our marriage."

"And if we sell our places in New York and Washington and buy the town house from him . . . what do you think?"

She didn't have to spend long at it. "He'd love it. *I'd* love it. But only if I can do the parlor over in white. I want warm and welcoming."

"You'll get virginal and forbidding."

"Trust me. It'll be warm and welcoming."

"It'll be filthy in a week."

"Only if you stomp through it wearing muddy boots."

"I won't. But what about the kids?"

She sucked in an audible breath and whispered, "The kids. That's an exciting thought. They can get the rug dirty. I don't care. You were right when you said they'll be beautiful. They will be."

He slid a hand to her tummy. "They may be right now. At least, the first of them."

She covered his hand to keep it there. "If we're sharing the Boston store, you can cover for me while I'm home with the kids. That way I could keep a hand in the till while they're little, but still have a career when they're grown."

"When they're grown, I want us to travel. Even before they're grown, I want us to do that." He urged her onto her side to face him, smoothed wisps of raven hair from her cheeks and left the backs of his fingers lightly caressing her skin. "I don't like the pace I've kept. I don't like the person I've been, working that way. Let's do things differently. Let's be more laid-back. We've each had our own store; we know the ropes. We should be able to do it with one eye closed by now. So we'll hire and train people to be the other eye. That way we'll have a real life."

Diandra liked that idea. She showed him so by smiling and turning her head just enough to kiss his fingers. She was feeling very relaxed, very laid-back indeed, which was why she was surprised when Greg said, "Let's get married tomorrow."

"Tomorrow?" So quickly! "I don't think we can. There's a waiting period—"

"Let's fly someplace where there isn't a waiting period. I want to be married, and I want it soon."

"But I want a big wedding. I've always wanted a big wedding."

"Then we'll have two. A secret one now and an unsecret one later."

"You're worried I'm pregnant."

"Not worried, because I'd be thrilled if you were, but it's something we should consider." His gray eyes were warm, yet they held an urgency. "There's been so much controversy between our families. I don't want anyone thinking, much less suggesting, that we had to get married. Because that's not true. You know it as well as I do. If we didn't feel what we do for each other, you'd never agree to the marriage, baby or no baby. And anyway, the possibility of a baby is only one reason to get married now. The other is that I don't want to risk losing you."

"You couldn't lose me."

"I almost did last weekend. I almost did this morning."

"But that was before we knew what we know. I love you, Greg. I'm not leaving."

He wasn't completely convinced. "We'll fight. We always have, always will. We're both capable of doing rash things in anger."

"Then we'll have to work on that. But I want a big wedding, and I want it in June. I'll elope with you tomorrow only if you'll let me have that."

"You've always dreamed of a big June wedding?"

"No. But I want the world to know who I'm marrying, and a big June wedding sounds like fun."

Greg realized that her argument worked both ways. He wanted the world to know who he was marrying, too. And besides, he was in a compromising mood. "Okay. We'll have two weddings. But if we go for the big shindig in June, we'll go for a big honeymoon afterward. What say you to a cruise to France, then a trip to the chateau of this renegade Frenchman, Charles de Montclair?"

She draped an arm over his shoulder. "I say that's very romantic."

"Could be less than luxurious if the chateau turns out to be a barn."

Diandra squeezed her eyes shut and wailed, "Don't ruin the image."

"But it could be so."

"So?"

"So the accommodations could be lousy."

"So?"

"So honeymoons are supposed to be posh."

She shook her head. "Honeymoons are supposed to be a time when husband and wife are together. We will be. I don't care where."

Splaying a large hand over her bottom, he pressed her close. "As long as there's a bed," he murmured and, dipping his head, sucked her lower lip into his mouth.

She didn't get it back for a while, and it was a while after that before she could gather enough breath to speak. Her head was on his chest, her leg fallen limply between his. "Greg?" she asked in a whisper.

He was lying on his back with one arm thrown to the side and the other resting along her spine. "Mmm?"

"Am I as good as Corinne?"

"Better. Much better." He paused. "Tommy Nolan?"

"No comparison."

"Him, or me?"

"You. He didn't know what he was doing. Or maybe it was me who didn't know what I was doing. It wasn't a particularly satisfying experience."

"I'm glad." Again he paused. "Diandra?"

"Mmm?"

"About our parents..."

"Hard to accept," she said in a small voice. "I know."

"I've thought one way for such a long time."

"Me, too."

"It may take a while to change."

"Mmm."

"Will you be patient?"

"If you will."

"I will."

They lay in silence for a time. Greg drew the blanket over them and shifted her more comfortably in his arms. Her face was nestled beneath his chin, in the spot she loved just below his beard.

"Greg?" she murmured against his skin. "Who do you think left the necklace on the mantel?"

"One of Bart's elves."

"Seriously."

"Seriously. He's a little bit of magic, that old man."

"And the necklace? Do you think it's magic?"

"I think it's suggestive. Maybe even seductive."

"I was worried that without it what we felt would fizzle, but last weekend in Washington, what I felt grew even stronger and the necklace was here."

Greg suddenly tossed the covers back, rolled to the side of the bed and was up.

"Where are you going?" she cried in alarm.

"To get it. It's still downstairs."

She put a hand to her throat, surprised to find it bare. She was still grappling with that discovery when Greg returned. Putting one knee on the mattress, he pulled her up, propped her against his thigh and fastened the emeralds around her neck. He traced the circle of gems with his hand, trailing his fingers slowly down her throat and over the last diamond fringe. When his eyes met hers, they were gray velvet and deep.

"You are," he breathed on a note of awe, "the one woman in the world who can wear this necklace with style. Legend may have it that it was made for another woman, but as far as I'm concerned it was made for you."

Diandra was feeling all warm and tingly inside. Lean muscles, long limbs and more than six feet of hair-spattered skin could do it to her every time. Actually, she realized, Greg did it whether he was naked or not. All he had to do was to look at her with those hungry gray eyes, and she was lost.

"What about Bart?" she asked distractedly.

Greg followed her down to the bed. "What about him?"

"Should we tell him the necklace did it?" she whispered.

Dipping his head, Greg drew a line with his tongue up her throat from the necklace to her chin. "That'd give him a thrill."

She rubbed his thighs with hers. "He's such a romantic."

"So are you." While his mouth did erotic things to her ear, his hand cupped her breast, thumb dabbing her taut nipple. "Did the necklace do it?"

"I don't...know...ah, Greg..." She slid her open palm down his front. "What do you...think?"

"No ... yes ... maybe ... harder, Di, oh, yes ..."

There was no more talk then, and the issue of the emerald necklace and its power remained unresolved, but somehow that didn't matter. What mattered was their love and the fact that it made them complete. A Casey would marry a York, just as Bart had hoped, just as fate had decreed. The legend lived on.

FEVER
Elizabeth Lowell

Lisa Johansen, world traveller, had tasted the exotic and seen the extraordinary. But when a rancher called Rye came into her life, he ignited a feverish desire foreign to her mind, her body—and her soul.

Rye was certain Lisa was like the gold-digging women in his past. He'd been burned before, and he vowed he would make no more mistakes. Still, the sweet sting of her kisses tempted him to madness, and he knew he'd gotten dangerously close to the flame. But it was too late—he was addicted to the fire.

"For smouldering sensuality and exceptional storytelling Elizabeth Lowell is incomparable."

Romantic Times (USA)

MIRA

DESIRES & DECEPTIONS
Jasmine Cresswell

Heiress Claire Campbell disappeared seven years ago, following a deadly fire in a cabin in Vermont. Unless she claims her fortune within the year, it will be lost to her forever.

Into a family determined to keep its secrets comes Dianna Mason, a woman who claims to be Claire Campbell for one reason—she desires justice. Ben Maxwell, protector of the Campbell's business interests, wants the truth. And that means doing everything in his power to prove that Dianna is just another impostor.

Could Dianna really be Claire? Would Ben's attraction to her compromise his loyalty to the Campbells? Would it prevent him from seeing the truth? Together would they be able to uncover the identity of a killer determined to finish what was started seven years ago?

"A brilliantly crafted romantic suspense"
Affaire de Coeur (USA)

MIRA

CRUEL LEGACY
Penny Jordan

One man's untimely death deprives a wife of her husband, robs a man of his job and offers someone else the chance of a lifetime...

PHILIPPA RYECART—when her comfortable, sheltered world collapsed around her, she was not prepared to play the grieving widow.

JOEL BRUTON—with his job on the line, he hungered for emotional—and physical—comfort. He was to find consolation in an unexpected alliance.

SALLY BRUTON—with the role of family breadwinner forced upon her, she was tragically unaware of her husband's need for her, although she *was* susceptible to another man's flattering attention.

DEBORAH FRANKLIN—young and impetuous, she was ready to move up the career ladder. But was there any truth in her lover's accusations that her promotion was based less on merit than on the fact that her womanising boss desired her?

One death touches all these lives. How well will each of them survive such a *Cruel Legacy*...?

MIRA